THE UNSTOPPABLE FLYING FLANAGAN

FELICE ARENA

T0364388

T0362735

PUFFIN BOOKS

THE UNSTOPPABLE FLYING FLANAGAN

Felice Arena is one of Australia's best-loved children's writers. He is the author and creator of many popular and award-winning children's books for all ages, including the acclaimed historical adventures *The Boy and the Spy*, *Fearless Frederic* and *A Great Escape*, as well as the bestselling Specky Magee books and the popular Besties, Andy Roid and Sporty Kids series.

PUFFIN BOOKS

For Sister Johanna, my first footy hero – FA

PUFFIN BOOKS

UK | USA | Canada | Ireland | Australia
India | New Zealand | South Africa | China

Penguin Books is part of the Penguin Random House group of companies
whose addresses can be found at global.penguinrandomhouse.com.

Penguin
Random House
Australia

First published by Penguin Random House Australia Pty Ltd, 2022

Text copyright © Red Wolf Entertainment Pty Ltd, 2022

The moral right of the author has been asserted.

Cover design and cover illustration by Astred Hicks, Design Cherry
Design © Penguin Random House Australia Pty Ltd
Printed and bound in Australia by Griffin Press, an accredited ISO AS/NZS 14001
Environmental Management Systems printer

A catalogue record for this
book is available from the
NATIONAL
LIBRARY
OF AUSTRALIA
National Library of Australia

ISBN: 978 1 76 104436 6 (paperback)

Penguin Random House Australia uses papers that are natural and recyclable
products, made from wood grown in sustainable forests. The logging
and manufacture processes are expected to conform to the
environmental regulations of the country of origin.

penguin.com.au

1942

At first it looks like a humpback whale breaching the surface of the water. A gigantic splash. Seawater fountaining high into the sky.

But it's not a whale.

It's a submarine.

Several men emerge from a cylindrical hangar at the front of the submarine. They hurriedly assemble a small plane. It has two seats and has floats underneath that mean the plane can sit on the surface of the water.

It's painted camouflage green. On the side is a large crimson-red disc.

In no time at all the plane is ready for take-off, the pilot strapped into the cockpit. He signals.

The propeller whirls and the engine buzzes. The plane zooms forward on the short runway, along the submarine's deck, and rises into the heavens.

The small aircraft heads northward over the deep waters of the Bass Strait.

It passes King Island unseen, and flies on towards Cape Otway. The pilot banks the plane northeast and follows the Australian coast.

It's dawn and the first rays of the summer sun flare in the pilot's eyes.

He continues to fly eastward, over Point Lonsdale lighthouse near the narrow entrance to Port Phillip Bay, and then on to Melbourne . . .

It's only just light. Enough light to kick a footy, even though the sun is hidden behind the clouds. Everyone's day starts early, but Maggie is always up before anyone else in her street. Otherwise there'd be no time for football training in the backyard.

'And the pacey centreman Harold Bray kicks it out towards the wing, where it's scooped up by Wilkie . . .' Maggie commentates, keeping her voice low so she doesn't wake Mum or the baby or her big sister, Rita, or let Dad know she's up.

There'll be jobs to do if Dad realises she's out of bed, but he won't see her through the back windows. They're covered with curtains and blankets nailed to the window frames so no light can be seen at night. If an enemy bomber flies in over Melbourne, there won't be any light to aim at.

'The little wingman bolts towards the forward line, easily outrunning the North Melbourne opponent. And here comes Keith Miller . . .'

Maggie twists and turns and ducks under the clothesline, crossing the narrow backyard. Her plaited ginger hair whips left, then right.

Their block isn't nearly big enough for booting fully extended kicks. Maggie has lost count of how many times she's thumped the footy into her neighbours' yards or the laneway that runs behind their plot.

'Miller leads for Wilkie's kick and marks the ball directly in front of the big sticks!' Maggie calls under her breath. 'Miller turns and takes his kick for goal, his sixth for the match, and . . . St Kilda forges ahead!'

Maggie kicks a rainmaker of a punt.

The footy seems to float mid-air for a couple of seconds before it spirals downwards. With her eye on the ball, Maggie jostles into position, nudging out her imaginary opponent, but now something else has caught her attention.

Something in the sky.

At first it's just a tiny speck breaking in and out of the clouds. But then Maggie hears a low drone that gets louder and louder. The speck gets bigger and bigger and now it's directly above.

The football falls.

THUD!

It bangs and bounces onto the tin roof of the dunny shed in the back corner of the yard.

But Maggie doesn't even notice the noise.

She can see a plane.

And even from a distance, she can clearly see the crimson-red disc on the side of the aircraft.

'Japanese?' she whispers. She has to hear herself say it to actually believe it.

And then . . .

'The enemy!' she yells. 'It's the Japanese! A Japanese plane!'

She bolts, ducks under the clothesline, smacks open the fly-wire back door and charges down the hallway.

'Dad! It's the Japanese! Wake up, Mum! We need to get to a bunker. Mr Gaffney's is closer, or should we go to the one at the end of the street? We're going to be bombed! The enemy is here!'

Maggie heads straight through the house and out the front door. Her mother and older sister pop their heads out of their bedrooms to see what all the commotion is about. Maggie runs into the street yelling. Alarmed neighbours stream out of their houses.

Dad follows her out. He's still in his pyjamas and

white singlet and has bits of shaving cream on his face.

'Maggie! What on earth are you doing?'

'The Japanese, Dad!' Maggie puffs. 'I saw them! A plane! Flying over us! We've got to take cover, quick fast!'

Maggie's father looks to the sky. 'There's no plane, Maggie. Nothing.'

He's right. The plane is gone.

'Is this some kind of game?' he says, perplexed, wiping the shaving cream off with his arm.

Maggie sighs, clasping her father's hand, wanting to drag him away from danger. 'No, Dad. It's not a game. I swear it was a Japanese plane. We can't just stand around. We'll be bombed just like they bombed Darwin.'

'Is everything all right, Joe? Is Maggie hurt?' It's Mrs Fitzgerald, their next-door neighbour. Her hair is still in curlers.

Maggie's best friend, Gerald, trails out after his mother.

'Oh, my, oh, my. What's all the commotion?' a voice says behind him.

It's his grandma, shuffling out onto the footpath in her flowery pink nightgown. The ruffled collar and her cat's-eye spectacles make her look like a character from an old storybook.

'Maggie says it's the Japanese,' Gerald tells her, taking her arm.

'Who has weak knees?' she says loudly.

'No, Nan!' Gerald says into his grandmother's good ear. '*Japanese*, not weak knees!'

Maggie can tell her dad is trying not to laugh. Some of the other neighbours already are. No one seems to be taking her seriously.

'Don't laugh! They could drop a bomb on us any minute.'

'Deary me,' says Mrs Fitzgerald, looking worried, turning her gaze skyward. 'Are you sure the plane was Japanese?'

'If it were the enemy, then we'd know about it. There would be air-raid sirens.'

It's Grumpy Gaffney from next door. Mr Gaffney fought in the last war. He lives alone, and Maggie has heard her mum say that his wife passed away years ago. Some days he's grumpier than others, like when Maggie kicks her football into his backyard. Maggie knows she has to stay on his good side, or she won't get her ball back next time.

Grumpy Gaffney limps out onto the kerb, waving his walking stick. 'As an official Air Raid Preparation warden, I'd be one of the first to get word of any imminent attack. We wouldn't be standing around like this if the situation were so perilous. And I don't appreciate high-pitched squealing at any time of day, young lady.'

'Maybe she was having some sort of nightmare?' says Mrs Fitzgerald, as if Maggie isn't standing right there. 'The girl is obviously traumatised by the news of last week's bombing of Darwin. We all are.'

Maggie wishes her big brother Patrick were there. *He* would believe her. And if anyone would know about planes, he would. Patrick enlisted with the Royal Australian Air Force on his nineteenth birthday, and he's been away for almost eighteen months. They're not allowed to know where he's been sent. All Maggie knows is that he's somewhere in the Mediterranean, fighting against the Germans and the Italians.

'It was definitely a plane,' Maggie tells everyone.

'Who's in pain?' Nan Fitzgerald says.

'No, Nan,' says Gerald. '*Plane*, not pain!'

'Come on, Mum,' says Mrs Fitzgerald. 'We'll head back in, now that we know it was a false alarm. Gerald, you've got to get ready for school.'

'I believe you, Maggie,' Gerald says as he helps Nan back into the house. 'I'll ask someone at the newspaper offices and some of the other newspaper boys. Someone else is sure to have seen the plane.'

'I think we're dealing with an over-active imagination,' Grumpy Gaffney says as he limps back to his house.

Maggie sighs. 'It's not a false alarm!'

'Let's go inside, Carrots,' her dad says, putting his arm around her. 'We'd better get on with the day. I'll ask about it once I get to work, all right?'

Maggie smiles. Only her dad and Patrick call her Carrots.

Her dad works as a clock winder in the city, winding and cleaning clocks at the train stations and at the Melbourne Town Hall. Maggie feels slightly relieved. He sees a lot of people during his workday. Surely someone else will have seen a plane flying over.

She can't be the only person in Melbourne to have seen something this serious.

Can she?

2

Waiting out front of Gerald's house, Maggie can hear the sounds of a piano and Gerald belting out a song from one of his favourite musicals, *The Wizard of Oz*. Maggie often thinks her best friend lives his life as if it were one big musical. He has a song for every moment and every emotion. And he's never afraid to sing them, even if it means he's going to get teased or get a whack from one of the other boys.

Maggie bounces her football in time with the rhythm of the music.

'Oi, Flanagan!'

It's Mickey Mulligan, looking scrappier than ever. He's in Maggie and Gerald's class at school, but neither of them would call him a friend.

'Thanks for screaming your head off at sparrow's fart and waking us all up. There's no way the enemy could make it this far. They would've been shot out of the sky. Hang on, what are you doing with that footy? Give it to me!'

Mickey goes to grab the footy, but Maggie side-steps him.

'You can't have it. It's Patrick's. He asked me to take care of it while he was away, and if you give me any trouble I wouldn't want to be in your shoes when he gets back home. I know what I saw, so mind your own business or I'll chuck this at your head.'

Maggie raises the football, ready to throw it at Mickey.

'I dare ya,' Mickey snarls. 'You couldn't anyway. Girls can't throw . . . and they sure can't kick.'

'That's what you think. I'm getting so good, and I'm going to get even better. When Patrick gets home, he'll be really impressed . . . and we'll kick-to-kick together.'

'In your dreams!' Mickey laughs. 'You shouldn't even be holding a football. It's unnatural!'

'Your head is unnatural,' Maggie says, as Gerald steps outside his front door.

'Morning, Mickey,' he says, cheerfully.

'Shut up, you namby-pamby mama's boy,' Mickey snaps back at him.

Then he turns and races ahead of Maggie and

Gerald in the direction of school.

'You shouldn't let him speak to you like that,' Maggie says, as she gently handballs the footy through the open front door of her house.

Gerald shrugs, side-stepping a pad of steaming manure left by the milkman's cart horse.

'How long have we known him? He always speaks to me like that.'

'Well, that doesn't make it right,' Maggie says, watching the ice delivery truck being parked across the street. 'Besides, he's getting meaner. If your dad or your brother were here, they'd never let him get away with it.'

To Maggie's surprise a woman hops out of the truck. With a pair of giant tongs, she grabs an ice block from the back. Slinging it over her shoulder, she delivers it to one of the houses in the street.

'Will you look at that?' Maggie says, impressed. 'The iceman is an ice-woman now. And she's driving!'

'I know,' says Gerald, crossing the road to grab some shattered ice chips from the back of the truck. 'Morning, Ivy!' he calls to the woman.

He pops the shards into his mouth and closes the back doors for her. 'Mr Canty enlisted,' he tells Maggie. 'He's gone to war. They couldn't find a man for the job so they hired Ivy. She's a friend of my mum.'

Ivy waves at Gerald and Maggie and drives farther down the street.

'Look!' Gerald whispers. 'Isn't that the boy you like – George Sullivan?'

Maggie looks across the street and sees a group of older boys running in their school sports kit.

George's eldest brother, Michael, is Patrick's best friend. They enlisted in the Royal Australian Air Force together. George is a few years older than Maggie and Gerald so he attends an all-boys college, but Maggie has seen him play footy for the school.

'No! I mean, yes! I mean, I don't *like* him. Not like that. Oh . . . never mind.' Maggie sighs.

But George has already seen them and is calling hello.

Maggie waves, as George drops back from the other lads and stops to talk. She can feel a blush heating up her cheeks.

Gerald notices and elbows her in the side, grinning. She elbows him right back.

'Where are you boys running to?' she asks George.

'We're not running to anywhere,' George says. 'We're training for St Patrick's Sports Day next month.'

'You had a smashing footy season last year,' Maggie says. 'I can't wait for the VFL to start. I bet you're chomping at the bit, too. You keep going the way you're going, and you'll be playing for St Kilda in no time.'

Now George is the one to blush.

'I don't want to speak too soon,' he says, running his fingers through his sandy hair. 'It might not go ahead this year anyway. More and more players are enlisting and heading off to the war. Melbourne and Collingwood are struggling to field their sides. They might even merge!'

'Do you really think we might not have footy this year?' Maggie says, horrified.

George nods. 'Some of the players have been injured or they're missing in action. Some of them who signed up early aren't coming home. Ronald Barassi was the first VFL player killed, but he won't be the last. I heard the VFL are talking about cancelling the season.'

'We've *got* to have footy. This city without football is like . . . um . . . birds without wings.'

'Or Glenn Miller without his band,' Gerald cuts in.

George grins. 'It sure is,' he says.

'Have you heard from Michael lately?' Maggie asks, hoping for some recent news of her brother. 'Did he mention Patrick?'

'Mum got a letter from him just before the new

year telling her about his time training in the desert somewhere. Dad says it's probably North Africa, but the censors blot out all the details so we don't know for sure. That was a while ago now. Michael said that Patrick was teaching the locals how to play footy.'

Maggie smiles. 'Sounds about right!' But talking about her big brother is making her feel sad and worried. 'We haven't heard from Pat for a while,' she says.

'Try not to worry. It can take months for the letters to come through. We haven't heard from Michael recently either. I'd better be off, or I won't catch the others,' George says. 'Bye, Maggie! Bye, Maggie's mate!'

'Bye, George,' Maggie calls after him.

'Yes, bye, George. Gorgeous George!' Gerald teases, mimicking Maggie. 'Oh, how you make my heart flutter. How you make my heart sing!'

—

At the school gates the nuns in their black-and-white habits greet everyone as they stream in.

'Good morning, children,' says Sister Agnes. 'I've made scones, so come and visit us in the convent at lunchtime if you'd like some.'

Sister Agnes is the oldest nun at their school. No one knows exactly how old she is. The first graders in the school think she's a hundred years old. Sister Agnes is always smiley to everyone. And, somehow, even though there are sugar rations, she manages to bake the most amazing sweets and cakes. Maggie detests baking cakes, but she does enjoy eating them.

'Walk, don't run!' bellows Sister Gertrude, the principal. 'I said walk, Mickey Mulligan! And tuck your shirt in and tie your shoelaces. I tell you this every day, and yet you insist on showing up looking like a hobo.'

Mickey turns, sticks his thumbs in his ears, wiggles his fingers and pokes his tongue out at Sister Gertrude.

'I can't believe he just did that,' Gerald whispers, shocked. 'Right in front of her.'

'I can,' says Maggie. 'Mickey's a shilling short of a pound. It's like he wants to get caned.'

Sister Gertrude marches over to Mickey, grabs him by the collar of his shirt and points him in the opposite direction to the classrooms.

'Right! Off to my office. It's the cane for you,' she growls, before she turns and catches Maggie and Gerald staring.

'Maggie Flanagan and Gerald Fitzgerald, stop

gawking and get a move on.'

Gerald grabs Maggie's arm and pulls her across the quadrangle, but Maggie can see their classmates Frances O'Brien and Nora Sweeney making a beeline for them. They're wearing matching emerald green ribbons in their hair.

'Oh, no. Don't look now, but Miss Prim-and-proper-and-I-know-it-all is heading this way,' Maggie says.

'Maggie, Mickey told us you were on the street this morning and you were in *absolute* hysterics,' Frances says, her hands on her hips. 'Is it true, Gerald?'

'Oh, no. I wouldn't say that,' says Gerald. 'She wasn't in hysterics.'

'Thank you, Gerald,' Maggie says.

'She was beside herself, frantic even. And she was bellowing in the street for everyone to hear. But I wouldn't say she was *hysterical*.'

Maggie glares at him and turns back to Frances.

'I saw a Japanese plane, and I tried to warn everyone.'

'Well, I think claiming to have seen the enemy is far from funny,' Frances says, raising her eyebrows at Nora. 'It makes a mockery of our boys in uniform and the dangerous work they do to defend our great country.'

'How dare you!' Maggie screws up her nose and

clenches her fists. 'You know my brother is over there too.'

Thankfully at that moment the school bell rings and everyone rushes to line up at the entrance of the red-brick school building. Still glaring at Frances, Maggie runs to join their classmates.

They all march inside in an orderly queue and drop off their cases and satchels in the hallway.

Some of the boys dawdle, loudly talking over each other. Frances and Nora take their seats together in the front row of the classroom.

'Good morning and God bless you, class,' Sister Clare says from her table.

'Good morning and God bless you, Sister Clare.'

There's a quiet knock at the door and everyone turns to stare. It's Elena Spinelli. Everything about Elena stands out. She's the only dark-eyed, dark-haired student in a sea of freckly, pale Irish-Australian kids.

She blushes and twists her plaits around her fingers. She's new to Maggie's school, having moved to Melbourne only a couple of weeks ago from the country.

'Please forgive me for being late, Sister,' she says in a quiet voice. She walks as quickly as she can to her desk, directly behind Maggie. 'The tram broke down and it took a while before they cleared it.'

'That's all right, Elena,' Sister Clare says.

As soon as their teacher turns to the blackboard, two of the boys whisper something. Maggie can't quite hear what it is, but she can tell it's nasty. Elena slides down in her wooden seat, like she's trying to make herself as small as possible.

The boys laugh.

Maggie scowls at them and shakes her head. She turns to Elena. 'Just ignore them,' she whispers. 'They have peas for brains.'

But Elena drops her gaze and doesn't respond.

Sister Clare scratches the date on the blackboard in chalk: *Thursday, 26th February, 1942.*

She spins round and faces her class, beaming. Maggie smiles back. It's hard not to. Sister Clare's twinkly eyes and kind round rosy face make everyone feel at ease.

But before Sister Clare can start the class, Mickey limps into the room. He waddles to his desk and winces as he settles his bottom on the seat.

'Sorry, Sister,' Mickey says. 'I had to, um, pay Sister Gertrude a visit. She said I should apologise to you for being late. So, um, sorry.'

Mickey's mate Jimmy Noonan leans into him.

'How many whacks?'

'Six,' Mickey says with gritted teeth.

'Strewth!' Jimmy says. 'Did ya cry?'

'No way. Crying's for babies. Didn't even feel it.'

'All right, enough, you two,' Sister Clare says. 'Maggie, could you please pass this to Mickey? Mickey, you can sit on this for the day.'

Sister Clare hands Maggie a small pillow from behind her table.

Maggie grins and throws the pillow at Mickey, but he reacts too slowly, and it hits him in the head.

'Oi!' he cries.

'Maggie!' Sister Clare frowns. 'I meant for you to take it to Mickey. Not toss it.'

'Sorry, Sister,' says Maggie. 'Mickey, I guess you were right when you said girls can't throw.'

Beside her, Maggie can see Gerald trying not to laugh.

3

'Now we're all here, I'm pleased to say we have a guest,' says Sister Clare.

Maggie turns to the door and sees Sister Gertrude standing there, next to a man she doesn't recognise.

'I have some big announcements,' says Sister Gertrude, marching into the room. 'So pay attention. Father Sheen has had a bit of a health scare and will be out of action for the next few weeks.'

Some of Maggie's classmates, including Mickey and Jimmy, hiss 'Yes!' but they freeze when Sister Gertrude whips her head around to glare at them.

'This is Father Finney,' says Sister Gertrude. 'He will be filling in for Father Sheen.'

Father Sheen is a crochety old grey-haired bore, and Maggie can't help noticing that the young priest standing beside Sister Gertrude is the complete opposite. For one thing, he's smiling. Father Sheen never smiles.

'He looks like Clark Gable,' Gerald whispers to Maggie. 'He should be in the pictures.'

Frances and Nora are whispering together too. It's obvious they're also taken by the new priest's film-star good looks.

'The best of the morning to you all!' the priest says in a thick Irish accent. 'I'm thrilled to be here, and I look forward to getting to know you all. First question. Can anyone tell me, if I take a potato and divide it into two parts, then into four parts, and each of the four parts into two parts, what would I have?'

Everyone looks confused. Frances has her hand in the air, desperate to be the first one to answer the mathematical question – to show off how smart she is. But the new priest replies before she gets a chance.

'I'd have potato salad!'

It takes a few seconds for everyone to realise that Father Finney has just cracked a joke. It's not especially funny, but everyone smiles anyway.

Only Sister Gertrude isn't amused.

'I've got another one,' adds Father Finney. 'What do you call the largest mammal on earth that lives in a palace? The Prince of Wales! Get it? Whales?'

This time everyone bursts into laughter.

'Settle down! You've had your fun,' Sister Gertrude snaps. 'Thank you, Father, for your, um, humour.'

Father Finney bows as if he's on a stage. 'Thank you, Sister. Everyone, I am pleased to announce that the Bishop has selected this school, specifically the Grades Five and Six classes, to run a fundraising event to raise money for the troops,' he says, clasping his hands together.

Everyone murmurs enthusiastically.

Sister Gertrude shushes them.

'It's indeed a grand honour to be chosen,' Father Finney exclaims. 'The fundraiser is to be held in just over two weeks, so I'd like you all to put your heads together and come up with an idea that is bold and exciting – and is sure to raise a lot of funds for our fighting boys.'

There's a long silent pause. Everyone is waiting for Father to continue. But he doesn't.

'Oh, you mean now?' says Sister Clare, jumping in. 'You'd like us to come up with ideas *now*?'

'Yes, Sister,' says Sister Gertrude. 'What do you think Father means? Yes, he means now! So, ideas anyone?'

Hands shoot up. It seems everyone has a suggestion to put forward. But they're not all good.

'What about a doll pageant?'

'An ant-squashing competition?'

'A chicken race?'

'A worm-wrestling contest?'

Sister Gertrude shakes her head firmly.

Frances and Gerald both shoot their hands up.

'Yes, Frances?' says Sister Gertrude, pointing at her.

'What about a cake and biscuit stall, Sister?' she suggests. 'We could bake with Sister Agnes.'

The boys groan. So does Maggie.

'Yes, I like that idea,' says Sister Gertrude. 'What do you think, Father?'

'A cake stall would be good, but rationing might make it difficult to find ingredients.'

'Then we could also have a sewing circle. We could all sew shirt buttons and stitch socks,' adds Frances, smiling proudly.

'Perfect for the girls,' says Father.

Maggie sighs. She hates sewing even more than baking.

'And you?' The new priest points at Gerald.

'What about a concert? We could all perform. I could sing. Something like this . . .'

Gerald bursts into the song *It's a Great Day for the Irish*. He has perfect pitch, and his joy for singing is infectious. Almost everyone starts to tap along.

A couple of the girls even start to sing too.

But Mickey leans forward and punches Gerald in the arm. Hard.

'Gerald Fitzgerald! That will do!' Sister Gertrude snaps. 'The classroom is no place for theatrics.'

'You have a fine voice, young man,' says Father Finney to Gerald. 'But we already have a parish concert planned for St Patrick's Day, so I think we need something else.'

Gerald slumps into his chair.

Maggie mouths, 'Sorry!'

But then she's struck with a brilliant thought.

'I know!' she cries. 'What about a charity football match?'

All the boys cheer, except Gerald.

Maggie notices that Elena looks up for the first time since the boys whispered at her.

'Perfect for the boys,' says Father Finney. 'Something for everyone.'

'No, I don't mean just for the boys,' Maggie says.

'Maggie Flanagan, if you think you're being comical, you're not,' Sister Gertrude snaps.

'Excuse me, Sister, I'm actually not. We could have our own game. An all-girls football match.'

Everyone starts talking at once.

'No way!'

'Are you mad?'

'Could you even imagine? Sheilas playing footy!'

'Ridiculous!'

'Flanagan, you belong in a circus!' yells Mickey.

'Enough!' hollers Sister Gertrude, slapping her palm down on Sister Clare's table.

Everyone freezes. Even Father Finney and Sister Clare flinch.

'Maggie, I do not tolerate nonsense and that is the most ludicrous thing to come out of a pupil's mouth in a long, long time. You are to sweep the convent verandah during your lunch break.'

Frances smirks.

This time Gerald mouths, 'Sorry!'

'What about a billycart derby too?' Jimmy says. 'We could race them down the Barkly Street hill. We could charge the public to watch.'

'Yes, yes!' says Father Finney, beaming. 'Another brilliant idea for the boys.'

When Sister Gertrude and Father Finney leave, Maggie and her classmates settle down to do some writing practice in their copy books. Everyone dips their pens into their ink bottles, concentrating hard, trying not to drip ink on the pages.

Maggie leans over to Gerald and whispers, 'It's so unfair. Why do you boys have all the fun?'

'Don't bring me into it,' he says. 'I don't especially like footy. Or billycarts.'

Maggie ignores him. 'I'm going to plan an all-girls football match. And no one is going to stop me.'

'How?' Gerald asks, carefully pulling his pen out of the inkwell.

Immediately a big blot of ink drops onto the paper. It looks like a dead fly.

Gerald sighs.

Maggie's mind swirls. She's not sure how.

Not yet, anyway.

4

Maggie is sweeping the convent verandah, humming to herself. She looks across the road at her school-mates enjoying their lunch break. They're darting back and forth on the quadrangle and the oval. Some of the boys from her class are playing cricket, while some of the kids from the lower grades are playing jump-rope and hopscotch.

'Oh, you poor dear. Sweeping again?' says Sister Agnes. She's holding a small bowl and a spoon. 'I made some stewed rhubarb. I saw you from the window and thought you might like some. But don't tell Sister Gertrude since you're in trouble.'

'Thank you, Sister,' says Maggie, putting the broom down and reaching for the bowl.

She spoons the sweet and tart rhubarb into her mouth and it makes her tastebuds tingle.

'It's delicious!' she says.

'I heard you were a bit of a rascal this morning,' Sister Agnes says. 'If you ask me, dear, I say, good for you. Stick up for what you believe in. I know you all think I'm ancient, but it wasn't long ago that most girls weren't even allowed to go to school. Girls like you have made a lot of change since I was young.'

Maggie isn't quite sure what to say. No one has ever said anything like that to her before.

Sister Agnes winks at Maggie and shuffles back into the convent with the empty bowl.

As Maggie returns to her sweeping, a football drops out of the sky, bounces right past her, and rolls behind some rose bushes. Maggie looks back towards the school to see Mickey and Jimmy running towards her.

'I'll get it!' Maggie cries, dropping the broom.

But before she's even off the verandah, Maggie hears a *thoomp*. She looks up to see the football spiralling back towards Mickey and Jimmy.

It's a thumping kick! One of the longest punts she's ever seen. None of the boys in her grade can kick the ball like that.

Maggie sprints towards the rose bushes to see who kicked the ball, but no one is there.

Even once she's finished sweeping, Maggie is still wondering about it. She goes to look for Gerald and finds him playing knucklebones with a couple of the Grade Five boys. He throws the jacks in the air and catches them on the back of his hand.

'All the sweeping done?' he asks, when he notices Maggie hovering nearby.

Maggie nods, and Gerald leaves the others to carry on playing and joins her. They wander through the schoolyard.

'I guess it's better than the cane,' she says, gazing up to the sky.

'You're still wondering about that Japanese plane, aren't you?'

'Yes . . . no . . . I don't know. My dad says he heard that a couple of hundred Japanese aircraft were involved in the attack on Darwin. They blew up all the ships in the harbour and all the airfields. So many people were killed . . .' Maggie sighs. 'No one saw *them* coming. What if two hundred of them suddenly appear over Melbourne? Or over Sydney or Brisbane? What then?'

Gerald shakes his head. 'I know. Last week the war seemed so far away, and now it doesn't,' he says. 'Mum says Singapore was Britain's biggest military base and the Japanese managed to capture it last month. She spoke to Dad yesterday and some of the terrible things he's heard about what's happening in Singapore now would make your blood run cold.'

'I don't want to know,' Maggie says. 'Don't tell me.'

She spots Elena reading under a tree. 'Look! I think we should try to get to know the new girl properly. She seems lonely. And Mickey and Jimmy are even meaner to her than they are to you. Maybe she'll be the first to join my football team.'

'You don't really believe you can arrange an all-girls football game, do you?' Gerald asks. 'I mean, not everyone is like you, Maggie. How are you going to side a full team, let alone two teams of girls?'

Maggie grins. 'By asking? I can't be the only girl in this school, or all of Melbourne for that matter, who secretly wishes they could play footy. Come on, let's go!'

Maggie runs over to Elena and Gerald follows.

'Hi, Elena,' Maggie says cheerily. 'What are you reading?'

Elena holds up her book. It's *Anne of Green Gables* by L. M. Montgomery.

'I haven't read that,' Maggie says. 'Is it any good?'

Elena shrugs.

'We thought maybe we'd keep you company,' Gerald says.

'I don't mind my own company,' says Elena. 'And

most people wouldn't want to be seen with me anyway.'

She turns slightly away from them.

'Um, I was wondering, since you like football . . .' Maggie begins to say.

Elena looks surprised. 'What? How do you know I like football?'

'I noticed you seemed interested when I suggested a charity football match. I'm still going to arrange an all-girls football game so I was wondering if you would play.'

'I thought we'd decided on a billycart derby, a bake stall and a sewing circle,' Elena says.

'We did,' says Gerald, rolling his eyes. 'But Maggie is being stubborn as usual. Once she gets something into her head it sticks there.'

'Well, I do like football,' Elena admits. 'My dad used to play for my town – for the Murchison Football Club. Go the green and gold! Actually, have you heard of Leo Dwyer?'

Maggie shakes her head.

'He used to play for North Melbourne. My dad played alongside him in a grand final a few years ago.'

'So I was right, then.' Maggie grins.

'Just because I like footy, doesn't mean I can play.'

'Maybe you'd like to try,' says Maggie. 'I could help

you learn. My brother taught me.'

Elena shakes her head. 'That's not the problem. Haven't you seen how they all treat me here? I'm already different. And as far as everyone is concerned, I'm the enemy. Italians, Germans and Japanese are the enemy, remember? Even if we've lived here our whole lives. Better not be seen with the girl with the stupid black curly hair and the Italian name!'

Elena grabs her book, jumps to her feet and marches off.

'Come back!' Maggie calls after her. 'You know who else has an Italian name? Ronald Barassi! The champion rover for Melbourne. May he rest in peace. And what about Cyril Gambetta? He won St Kilda's best player in nineteen twenty-five! Barassi and Gambetta, you can't get more Italian than that . . .'

'You can stop now, Maggie,' Gerald says gently. 'She can't hear you. She's gone.'

Maggie sighs. She feels awful.

And then . . .

5

THOOMP!

A football whacks Gerald in the side of his head. It seems to have come from nowhere.

He groans, cupping his cheek.

Maggie looks around. Mickey and Jimmy are racing their way. They're both laughing.

'Nice shot,' Mickey crows. 'Take that, Vera Lynn!'

'Peas for brains!' Maggie says. 'That's the last straw. I'll get them, Gerald.'

She scoops up the footy with one hand and charges off with it.

'Maggie, just leave it,' Gerald cries. 'I'll be fine.'

'Drop it! That's ours!' Mickey shouts. 'C'mon, Jimmy.'

Maggie runs as fast as she can across the school oval, but Mickey and Jimmy are closing in.

Maggie picks up the pace, her plaits streaming behind her.

'And the little champ for St Kilda breaks away from the pack . . .' She can hear the usual commentary in her head, but this time it's a bit different. 'The little wingman is faster than ever. She charges towards the forward pocket! That's right, ladies and gentlemen, I said "she". Flying Flanagan is unstoppable. She's running rings around the chaps. She bounces . . . once, twice . . . There are only minutes remaining in this final quarter. Flying Flanagan spots her teammate, her big brother, Patrick "Fearless" Flanagan.'

Mickey sprints out in front of Jimmy. He is now only inches away from Maggie.

'Flying Flanagan disposes of the footy and kicks the perfect pass on to Fearless Flanagan. The crowd are beside themselves!'

Mickey lunges at Maggie and tackles her to the ground. The two hit the turf with an almighty *thud*.

Maggie feels the breath knocked out of her, and then a sudden pain as Mickey pushes his knee forcefully into her back. Then he jumps up and runs after the ball.

Maggie groans and grimaces. Her entire body is stinging, and her kneecaps feel as if they are on fire.

She wobbles back to her feet. Her legs are grazed and bleeding. And she's seething. She's not going to let Mickey get away with it. She bolts off again, chasing him like a cheetah running down its prey.

'Look out!' Jimmy warns Mickey. 'She's behind you!'

But it's too late. Maggie throws herself onto Mickey, and again they hit the ground.

'A knee in the back is just plain dirty,' Maggie says angrily, pinning him down.

'Get off me!' Mickey cries, trying to shake her off.

'Not until you say sorry to Gerald, you drongo.'

'Stop it! Stop this at once,' cries a voice. Maggie looks up and realises that everyone in the school yard has circled around her and Mickey.

Sister Clare reaches down to pull them apart. 'You two! On your feet now!'

'She nicked our football, Sister,' Mickey spits.

'They kicked it into Gerald's face,' Maggie says angrily. 'And they called him Vera Lynn, Sister.'

'I didn't really mind that part,' Gerald says, pushing through the crowd. 'If anything, I see that as a compliment. She's fabulous. One of my favourite British performers . . .'

'Please, Gerald.' Sister Clare sighs. 'Mickey, you'll apologise to Gerald and, Maggie, this had better not happen again because next time –'

'What do you mean next time?' roars a voice from behind everyone.

It's Sister Gertrude. The crowd parts around her as she marches towards them.

'Everything's under control, Sister,' says Sister Clare. 'These two were just about to apologise to each other and I –'

'It's clearly *not* under control,' Sister Gertrude says, cutting Sister Clare off. 'I saw everything from my window. Maggie Flanagan, I'm appalled! This is not how a young lady is supposed to act. What has come over you today?'

'It might have something to do with the Japanese spy plane she claims to have seen this morning, Sister,' Frances calls out, smirking. 'So she's also been telling lies.'

Maggie's heart is racing. Don't cry, she thinks. Don't you dare cry.

'I'm no liar, you stuck-up cow,' she mutters.

Everyone gasps.

'Right, I've had enough. It's the cane for you,' exclaims Sister Gertrude. 'To my office now!'

6

Maggie sits in Sister Gertrude's office, feeling sick.

Behind the principal's desk hangs a large gold-framed picture of an old man in a red cape. He's staring off into the distance, wearing a white skull cap and wire-rimmed glasses. But another, smaller painting catches Maggie's attention. It's a portrait of Mary, Jesus' mum. She's draped in blue cloth, with a hand on her heart. Maggie feels as if Mary is staring right at her, looking very disappointed.

'I really didn't do anything wrong,' she whispers. 'All right, maybe I shouldn't have called Frances a stuck-up cow or Mickey a drongo, but both those things are true. So I didn't lie. I know that Sister Gertrude works for God, but you're Jesus' mum so if there's some way you can get him to stop Sister Gertrude from giving me the cane that would be very much appreciated. And I want to play football, so could you please help me to find other girls who would like to play? Oh, and could you protect Pat and his squadron? I think that's all. Thank you for your time. Amen. Or maybe that should be A-women. Get it?'

Maggie thinks about her prayer. She's pretty sure getting out of being caned isn't the kind of prayer that usually gets answered.

'I'm going to have to figure out a plan myself,' she mutters.

Maggie scans the room. On the desk is a pile of slim prayer books with leather covers.

She grabs one, and quickly shoves the book down the back of her skirt. She brushes down her skirt and looks back up to the portrait.

'Good idea, right?' She winks at Mary, just as Sister Gertrude marches in and startles her.

Sister Gertrude moves to the other side of her desk, opens the top drawer, and takes out a cane – a stick about fifty centimetres long.

Maggie starts to feel afraid again. What if the plan doesn't work?

'Right, turn around and bend over,' Sister Gertrude orders. She looks menacing.

Maggie takes a deep breath.

'I will not tolerate backtalk, name-calling or a combative attitude,' Sister Gertrude says. 'Especially not from girls. And suggesting that cockamamie notion about girls playing football was also out of order. You will learn to act like a lady.'

Sister Gertrude whips back the cane and swings it quick and fast.

Whack!

Maggie winces. But nothing. No pain!

She tries not to grin. The book is working. It's the perfect shield.

She pretends to cry out in pain.

Whack!

Whack!

Whack!

Maggie tries to squeeze some tears out, but she's not that good an actor. She scrunches up her face instead.

One more whack to go and she's free!

'Excuse me, Sister,' comes a voice from the door. 'There are some visitors from the Army at the front gate. I thought I'd better let you know.'

It's the school nurse, Nurse Nancy. Her young voice cracks a bit as she sees Maggie and the cane.

'Right,' says Sister Gertrude, placing the cane on her desk, and turning back to Maggie. 'Go to your class now and consider yourself very lucky. I'll be watching you like a hawk, Maggie Flanagan.'

Sister Gertrude leaves the office and Maggie lets out a huge sigh of relief.

'You look all right for someone who's just had four of the best,' Nancy says. 'There are usually a few tears. What's your secret?'

Maggie doesn't know the nurse that well. She's never been ill and never had a reason to visit her. But Nancy seems to be onto her, and she doesn't seem angry, more intrigued.

Maggie shrugs, and decides to take the risk. She pulls the little book out of the back of her skirt. 'Just the power of prayer,' she says, popping it back on the desk.

Nancy laughs. 'Well, you'd better get back to the classroom before you get a few more. But before you go, I heard two of the girls saying that you're wanting girls to play football? What's all that about?'

Maggie tells Nancy about her idea.

'Is it really so bad that I want to play footy?' she asks.

Nancy grins. 'One of the greatest days of my life was when I played football at Princes Park,' she says.

'What?' Maggie says. 'You actually played football? When? How?'

41

Nancy nods, still beaming. 'I played in the Royal Melbourne Hospital charity game for the Carlton football club in nineteen thirty-three. Gosh, I can't believe it – that's almost nine years ago now.'

'Go on,' Maggie says. 'Tell me about it! Please!'

'All right. We were split into teams, Carlton and Richmond,' says Nancy. 'It was a low-scoring game . . . but the crowd loved it. It was an incredible feeling. And we raised a lot of money – all our collection tins were full!'

Maggie shakes her head in disbelief.

'Did you play any more games?' she asks.

'No.' Nancy sighs. 'We were just a novelty on carnival day. The men had a good laugh at our expense, but we were deadly serious. Many of us wanted to start a women's league, but our dads and husbands wouldn't have a bar of it. They still won't, Maggie. Football's a man's game in a man's world. And I'm afraid it might be like that forever.'

'Play for *my* team!' Maggie says excitedly. 'If I can arrange a match, will you play? And could you ask some of your old teammates to play too?'

Nancy considers it for a minute.

'I don't know how you're going to do it, Maggie, but I'm sure there are a couple of my friends who will jump at the chance. Now, get to class before you-

42

know-who comes flying in on her broomstick and starts waving her cane.'

Maggie laughs. 'Was it you?' she asks. 'Did you kick a football from behind the rose bushes at the convent earlier?'

'No. I'm not sure what you mean, but it wasn't me,' Nancy says. She waves and leaves the room.

Maggie looks up at the small painting of Mary.

'I sorted the cane out myself, but Nancy is a very good start for a football team,' she says. 'Thank you, Mary. You're the best.'

7

'Dinner's ready!'

Maggie drops the footy and runs for the kitchen.

Her baby sister, Colleen, has been fed already and is happily playing with blocks on the floor. The front door slams.

'Is that you, Rita?' calls their mum. 'That's a long day.'

Rita left school at fifteen and was training to be a dressmaker with her friend Judith, but when the war started they began working at the Commonwealth Clothing Factory in the city making military uniforms.

She swans in, looking flushed and distracted. She takes out a couple of pins from her hair, and lets it drop onto her shoulders.

'If I see another stitch, I'll utterly lose my mind,' she says.

'You did that years ago,' Maggie teases.

'Oh, shut up,' says Rita.

'Girls, enough!'

'Mum, please. I'm not a girl anymore,' Rita exclaims. 'I'm almost nineteen.'

'She's a sophisticated laaaaady now, who's in love with Terry,' Maggie teases some more. 'And when she's twenty they'll get married. Ooooh!'

'Why, you little so-and-so,' Rita says. 'Terry and I will never marry.'

'What?' their mum says, surprised. 'But I always thought you two . . .'

'For your information, Mother, Terry and I are just friends. We've always been friends. That's it. And besides, he's about to head to Army camp, and there are other fish in the sea.'

Maggie's father walks into the room, shaking his head, and sits at the table.

'Stop baiting your sister, Carrots. Maybe we could eat in silence?' He digs his fork into his corned beef.

'Joe!' Maggie's mother says, slapping his hand. 'Maggie, could you say grace?'

Maggie and her family all stop and bow their heads.

'Bless us, O Lord, and these thy gifts, which we are about to receive from thy bounty, through Christ our Lord,' Maggie recites. 'Please look over Pat and all those fighting to keep our country safe and free. Amen.'

As everyone echoes 'Amen', Maggie whispers under her breath, 'A-women'.

Maggie's father spears a potato. 'I heard today that more rationing is planned,' he says. 'There'll be less food on the table for us all. I also heard that many of the boys fighting in Europe will be sent closer to home. With enemy attacks on Australia, we need them back here.'

Maggie's dad always talks about the war at the dinner table. Maggie listens intently and often finds herself wondering whether or not he feels left behind. She wonders if he feels that he should be fighting overseas, as he did in the Great War. He's too old to enlist now, and he sometimes walks with a painful limp so they wouldn't let him go anyway, even if he were younger.

He's never told Maggie what happened, but Patrick told her that in the last war the men had to live and fight in cold and muddy trenches with no dry socks or shoes for months. After a while, it did something terrible to the skin and nerves in their feet.

Patrick said it even killed lots of people or they had to have their feet chopped off to save their lives.

And if Maggie's mum ever fusses over her dad, he says, 'Let it go, love! It could've been worse; I could've lost them completely or come home in a box.'

'If they're coming back here, does that mean we'll see Pat?' she asks hopefully.

'It might,' her dad replies. 'It's time to protect our own territory. They're expecting thousands of Americans to be deployed here very soon too. They'll use Australia as a base.'

'I know!' Rita says excitedly. 'There are so many of them in Brisbane and now they're coming down here. They're setting up over in Parkville. They're so handsome and charming and tall.'

Maggie catches her father frowning at Rita with disapproval.

'Now we know why she's dropped the idea of marrying Terry,' Maggie says.

Rita pinches Maggie on the arm and glares.

Maggie makes a face at her sister and then asks her father if he has heard anything about the enemy plane.

'I talked to a fella who claims he saw a plane this morning, but he didn't say it was Japanese. Maybe you thought it was Japanese because of the glare of the sun or the reflection on the wing made it look like a red disc.'

Maggie sighs. She knows what she saw, and it was definitely an enemy aircraft.

'How was school?' her father asks.

There's no way Maggie is going to tell them how she got in trouble with Sister Gertrude. Or about her plans to arrange an all-girls football match. She's sure that her parents, especially her mother, would put a stop to that immediately.

Maggie shrugs. 'It was all right.' She tells them about the new priest and the fundraising events.

'Wonderful! A sewing circle and baking stall are a great idea,' says Maggie's mother as she collects everyone's plates. 'And the billycart derby for the boys should be fun, too. I'm looking forward to Mass this Sunday. I've heard that new priest is quite dashing – and from Ireland!'

Maggie's father rolls his eyes.

'Well, I'm off again,' Rita announces, pulling some red lipstick out of her purse. 'I'm meeting some of the girls from work at Judith's place. We're going to practise our dance steps. There's a new dance venue opening in the city soon and I can't wait.'

'Don't be out too late,' their dad calls after Rita, even though she's already headed for the door. 'Remember the brown-out. It will be very dark with no streetlights and the windows all covered so be careful, please.

And do you really think dancing is appropriate during these difficult times?'

'Oh, Joe, let her be.' Maggie's mother sighs. 'She works hard. She needs to let her hair down a little. And, besides, it's not all dancing. She and her friends are knitting scarves for the Red Cross.'

Maggie tunes out and heads to the backyard to play with the footy while it's still light out. Soon she can hear her parents laughing at their favourite wireless radio show, *Dad and Dave*, and occasionally Baby Colleen crying and being sung to by her mum.

The same sounds are coming from all the little houses squashed up close to each other on the street. Somewhere, someone is whistling and from next door she can hear Gerald playing piano.

Everyone in Gerald's family is musical. Before Gerald's brother and his dad were sent up to the bush for the war effort, it was like there was a whole concert band next door.

Gerald's father is a talented cornet player and Gerald says that his brother, Tony, can play the clarinet as well as the famous American clarinettist Benny Goodman. But they're both Army officers and they're based at a military training base in Puckapunyal in Northern Victoria so Gerald never gets to see them.

Soon Mrs Fitzgerald's beautiful singing joins the piano music.

Maggie smiles as she tosses the ball on a slanted section of the roof of the house and waits for it to bounce off. It's the perfect way to practise her marking, even if it's a bit loud. Over and over the football ricochets off the roof, and each and every time Maggie positions herself under it and marks it firmly in both hands.

'And Col Williamson gets it out of the centre and boots it on to Reg Garvin, who almost loses it. Garvin passes it off to Jack Kelly. Yes, folks, Kelly might not be as fast as Bray, but he certainly shows as much vigour . . .' Maggie commentates to herself as she turns and runs to the back of the yard. 'St Kilda is unstoppable today . . . especially now that Flying Flanagan joins the pack. She boots it on to Ken Walker, who wastes no time getting the ball into the skilful hands of Bill Mohr. Mohr lets loose with one of his famous drop kicks and . . .'

Maggie drop kicks the ball, but she misjudges how hard she kicks it.

It sails across the yard, across the clothes line, across the side fence . . . and *thoomp* into Grumpy Gaffney's yard.

She runs to the fence, climbs up on the cross beams and looks over.

Grumpy Gaffney is on his knees by his vegetable patch, weeding. Maggie's ball lies beside him.

'Sorry, Mr Gaffney!' Maggie cries.

'How many times have I told you to stop kicking the footy into my yard?' says Grumpy Gaffney, his bushy eyebrows scowling. 'I've had enough. The next time it happens, I'm going to puncture it.'

With that, Grumpy Gaffney throws the ball back over the fence.

'Thank you, Mr Gaffney,' Maggie says. 'And I really am sorry. But please don't puncture it. Patrick would be so upset. Do you really not like football? You must be the only man in Melbourne who doesn't.'

But Grumpy Gaffney doesn't respond. He kicks off his boots on the back step, walks inside and slams the door shut.

—

Later that night, as Maggie begins another letter to Patrick, she hears Rita's voice outside in the street. Maggie hops out of bed and peeks through the curtains and around the heavy blanket over the bedroom window.

She can't make out who Rita's talking to, but it's definitely a man's voice. She can only make out a tall silhouette in the moonlight. Whoever it is, he's making Rita giggle.

A few minutes later Rita quietly closes the front door and tiptoes into the room, holding her shoes in her hand.

The sisters share a bedroom, and Maggie tries not to be upset whenever Rita begs her parents to allow her to move into Patrick's room. Giving Rita his room feels like admitting that he might not come home.

'It should be left as is for his return,' Maggie's mother always replies.

'Why are you still up?' Rita asks, looking as guilty as a fox leaving a chicken coop.

'Who was that you were with?' Maggie teases. 'It didn't look like your friend, Judith.'

'Mind your own business,' Rita says, sitting down at the dresser to take her makeup off.

'I was writing to Pat,' Maggie says. 'But I was also waiting up for you because I want to ask you a favour.' Maggie tells her sister about her football plans.

Rita laughs and slips into bed.

'Well?' asks Maggie.

'Well, what?' Rita says. 'Why are you telling me about your crazy idea?'

'Could you please ask the girls you work with if

they would like to play football?'

Rita reaches over to the goose-neck copper lamp on the table between their beds.

Its dim light clicks off.

'Don't be silly. I will not embarrass myself. And neither should you.'

Maggie snaps her bedsheet over her head and sighs. This was going to be harder than she thought.

8

Once again, Maggie is awake at the crack of dawn.

As usual, she's woken by the sound of the milk-man's horse clip-clopping in the street out front. She loves horses – and her heart skips a beat every time she hears it approaching.

She quietly hops out of bed, so as not to wake Rita, gets dressed quickly, scoops up her football, and steps outside. She looks up at the sky, and for a moment she half expects to see the plane. But there's nothing in the dawn sky but clouds.

She waits outside the gate on the footpath, keen to ask the milkman whether he saw the plane yesterday. It's not until the milk cart stops in front of Gerald's house that Maggie realises that it's not the usual milkman – it's a milkwoman!

'Good morning,' says the young woman, waving.

'You're the first up in the street.'

'You're not Mr Stewart,' Maggie says, as she runs out to pat the cart horse's soft brown nose. 'I mean, sorry – where's Mr Stewart?'

'He enlisted last week,' says the woman. 'I'm Mrs Stewart. I'm taking over the milk run until he returns. We've all got to do our bit for the war effort, right?'

Maggie nods. Yesterday, Ivy the ice-truck lady. And today a milkwoman!

'I'm Maggie. My dad says more and more women are doing men's jobs,' Maggie says. 'He says that while the men are overseas fighting, women are holding down the fort. And we should all thank our lucky stars for that.'

The woman smiles. 'Too right! Smart man, your dad. Call me Marian,' she says. 'I just got married, and I'm still not used to the Mrs. It makes me think of my mother.'

Maggie grins. 'Did you see anything unusual on your milk run yesterday, Marian? I mean, did you happen to see a plane fly over around this time?'

Marian shakes her head. 'This is my first day on the job. Sorry, Maggie.'

Maggie notices a pin on Marian's collar, and all thoughts of the spy plane are immediately gone.

It's a small badge with the words *St Kilda Football Club* engraved on it, and beneath that is an image of a seagull. Only diehard fans call the Saints the 'Seagulls'. It's a name the club tried a few years back, but it didn't stick.

Maggie's mind is spinning.

'Marian,' she says, excitedly. 'Think fast!'

Maggie handpasses her footy to Marian. Without flinching, she grabs it with both hands.

'I knew it!' Maggie squeals. 'You can play footy!'

Marian laughs. 'Lucky I didn't have your milk bottle in my hands,' she says, deftly handpassing the ball back.

Maggie tells Marian about her idea to organise a game and asks her whether she would consider playing. 'It would be raising funds for the troops. Please, Marian. Please play!'

'I can't believe I'm saying this, but if you can actually field a side – two sides! – then count me in. I used to have a kick-to-kick with my dad, even if the other fathers in my street used to tease him about it. I was the son he never had.'

She grabs a bottle of milk from the back of the cart and places it at Maggie's feet. 'I don't know what my husband would think of it all, but he's not here, is he? Keep me updated, Maggie. I best be off now. Bye!'

Maggie and Gerald are sitting beside each other in a pew in the school's church. Their class sits in silence around them, waiting for their weekly confession. One after the other, they walk quietly to the back of the church and step into a booth with a seat in it and a little screened window to the booth next door. Father Finney will be sitting there to listen to them tell him their sins.

Frances brushes past Maggie on her way to confession. Jimmy walks back to the group, looking bored.

'I bet Jimmy had a lot to say,' Gerald whispers. 'I haven't done anything wrong lately. I'll have to make something up.'

'Ha! So you're going to lie about not doing anything wrong? Good one, Saint Gerald! I've got plenty to say this week. When are you going to start building your billycart for the derby?'

'I'm not sure where to start. I've never made anything before. Maybe your dad could help me,' Gerald whispers.

'It's not that hard,' says Nora, turning around from the pew in front of them. 'A couple of bolts, some screws, a crate and four old pram wheels and you'll be on your way.'

Gerald looks at Maggie in surprise. Nora rarely says anything. She follows Frances around like a shadow, nodding and agreeing with everything she has to say. But Frances is in the confessional booth now, and Nora is like another person.

'Um, thank you,' says Gerald. 'You could help me, if you like. I'm not really that keen to build one.'

'Really?' Nora perks up. 'I would love that. My brothers are ace billycart drivers. I wish I was allowed to race too.'

'But you were all for the sewing and cake stalls,' says Maggie.

'That was Frances more than me,' Nora says. 'I'm up next, but please don't tell Frances I'm helping you. She won't like it.'

Gerald nods and Nora leaves to tell the priest her sins for the week.

'I wonder if she's going to confess that to Father Finney,' Maggie says.

'Maggie!' Sister Clare turns around with a finger to her lips. 'It's a sin to talk in church.'

Maggie sighs.

Not another one!

9

'Are girls allowed to play football in Ireland, Father?' Maggie asks hopefully, wriggling on the velvet kneel-board.

'Not really, but if they were, my sister would be first in line. I've become a big fan of Australian Rules footy since then too.'

'Which VFL team do you barrack for, Father?' Maggie asks.

'I'm not sure the confessional is the right place for a chat about football,' Father Finney tells her. But Maggie can hear the smile in his voice. 'All right, this is *my* confession,' he says. 'I'm a Melbourne supporter. Go the Demons!'

'What? Fair dinkum?' Maggie squeals.

Father Finney shushes her.

'Why the Demons?' Maggie whispers. 'I mean, they're a great team and all. And they've won the last two premierships but, Father, if a priest is going to barrack for any team it should be the Saints, right? Not the Demons. Does God even allow that?'

This time Father Finney laughs.

'You make a good point,' he says. 'But Melbourne weren't always called the Demons. They were called the Fuchsias up until about a decade ago. A fuchsia is a flower. Not devilish at all. In the middle of last year, I saw my very first VFL match at the MCG. It was the

Patriotic Premiership carnival. I decided I would go for the first team I saw win that day – and that was Melbourne. Then I roared my heart out for them to the final game, the premiership, against Collingwood. They lost by only one point! Norm Smith, Ron Baggott and Allan La Fontaine were absolute champions.'

Maggie knows all about the Patriotic Premiership carnival. It's a knockout competition in which all the VFL teams play short games in one day. She went to the first one a year and a half ago, just before Patrick left for Air Force training. It was her first time at the MCG.

Along with her big brother and thirty thousand other spectators, she cheered St Kilda to a lightning premiership.

But even though her beloved team had won, she ended the day in tears. She remembers how much she wished Patrick wouldn't leave, how much she wished she could stop time forever that day. Now she wishes that life could go back to how it was, before fathers and uncles and brothers were sent off to training camps and battlegrounds in foreign lands.

Despite the sad memories, Maggie feels happy to be having such an unexpected conversation with a fellow footy fan, even if he is a priest from Ireland.

Suddenly a high-pitched hollow sound echoes around the church. The sound repeats over and over in a constant loop.

It's the air-raid siren.

Maggie's heart races.

'All right, Maggie. You know what to do . . . hurry!' orders Father Finney.

Maggie bursts out of the confessional booth. Everyone is already huddled under the church pews. There's room next to Elena so Maggie slides in on the cold stone floor.

She hopes it's only a drill. They've had two since the beginning of the school year.

'Elena?' she says, but she has her hands clasped over her head. 'Elena!'

'What?' she snaps.

'I just want to say I'm sorry. I'm sorry you feel so out of place and different to everyone else. I know people aren't very nice. It's not fair. If you do ever want to kick the footy with me, you can. And I already have a couple of interested players in the match. Isn't that great?'

'Maggie, shush!' Sister Clare calls out, looking at her from under the pews. 'There wouldn't be any time for chit-chat if bombs were falling.'

'If a bomb dropped, Sister,' says Maggie, 'I don't

think these benches would save us, no matter how much talking we're doing.'

Sister Clare shakes her head and sighs. 'True, but please, please be quiet because benches won't save you from Sister Gertrude either.'

Maggie looks back to Elena, but she's turned away, and has crawled under the next pew.

10

'If you meet me Saturday morning at St Kilda train station around eleven, we can finally go to the pictures together,' Gerald says to Maggie as they walk home from school. 'I can't wait to see *The Wizard of Oz* again. I just love that it's in colour! And Judy Garland is smashing in it.'

Gerald steps out ahead of Maggie, does a little tap-dance routine and bursts into song.

'Look at you!' Maggie giggles, as Rita rides up on her bicycle alongside them.

'G'day, you two!' she says, smiling. 'You still have all the moves, Gerald. Or should I call you Fred Astaire?'

'I answer to both.' Gerald beams, striking a *ta-da!* pose. 'I wish I were old enough to go dancing with you, Rita. And can I say *you're* looking more like a Hollywood star every day.'

'Why, thank you, Gerald,' says Rita, hopping off her bike and rolling it along as she walks beside them. 'As it turns out, I'm going dancing next weekend – to the opening of a new dance hall in the city. I can't wait!'

Maggie rolls her eyes and asks her sister why she's not at work.

'Because we had an electrical malfunction, and we were told to take the rest of the day off. So I decided to go for a ride . . .'

'And visit your mystery companion?' Maggie asks, grinning.

'You have a lot of cheek, you know that?' Rita says.

But Maggie doesn't hear the rest of what Rita has to say. Something has caught her attention. Someone on a bicycle, riding past. She can't believe it. It's St Kilda champion Harold Bray. She grabs her sister's arm.

'What? What's going on?' Rita cries.

'That . . . that . . . that was Harold Bray,' Maggie says in disbelief.

Rita shrugs as if to say 'Who?'

'Do you mean the footballer?' Gerald says.

'Argh! Of course the footballer!' Maggie says, grabbing Rita's bicycle and hopping on it. 'But he's not just any footballer. He's going to be one of the greats of all time, mark my words! There's no other centreman in the league like him.'

Maggie crunches down on the pedals and takes off after her footy hero.

'Where do you think you're going?' Rita hollers.

'I'm off to meet Harold Bray,' Maggie shouts back, already halfway down the street.

Maggie has the young champion in her sights. But she hasn't ridden a bicycle this fast before.

There are hardly any cars on the street, most of Maggie's neighbours can't afford to own their own automobile, but Maggie overtakes an Oldsmobile and a Chevrolet sedan. There are no new cars anyway, since the war started. The idea that her family might own a car seems like a dream.

Her heart is thumping, her legs are pumping, and her mind is spinning wildly. She's not sure what she'll say to Harold Bray when she catches up to him. She once saw him play for Prahran in the VFA, and then cheered for him last season, his first for the VFL. She'd yelled with excitement every time the commentators on the wireless called out his name.

I wonder if I could get him to write something? Maybe a message for Patrick? she thinks, standing up out of her seat, pumping her legs up and down on the pedals. Pat won't believe it!

'Mr Bray!' Maggie calls out.

Her eyes are still firmly fixed on him. She picks up her pace some more. He takes a sharp left and whizzes out of sight. Maggie grits her teeth and turns the corner. She overshoots the bend and takes a wide turn out into the other side of the road, right in front of an ice truck.

The truck veers off the road to miss Maggie, slightly onto the edge of the street, narrowly missing several pedestrians. But Maggie loses her balance, and before she knows what's happening, everything is a blur.

She feels her leg and shoulder hit the road. *Thump!* A sharp pain shoots through her.

She's lying there stunned when she sees Ivy the ice-truck driver looking over her. Other people rush to her side. Another woman picks up the bicycle and wheels it off the road.

'Are you all right?' Ivy asks, kneeling down. 'Don't move. Did you hit your head?'

Maggie says no.

Ivy feels her arms and legs, but nothing hurts enough to be broken.

'You're Gerald's friend! I saw you yesterday,' says Ivy. 'You'll need to clean those grazes. You look an absolute sight.'

Maggie looks down to see her long white socks scuffed and part of her skirt torn – her shins and palms sting. They're bloody and grazed.

Feeling wobbly on her feet, Maggie limps to the kerb. Ivy darts back to the truck and returns with a flax canvas water bag and a couple of icy shards she has scraped off the ice blocks packed inside the back of the truck.

She hands the shards to Maggie, who cups them in her hands. The cold soothes her burning, bruised palms.

'Thank you.' Maggie sighs. 'I'm so sorry!'

Ivy pours water onto Maggie's knees and washes the pieces of gravel out of the grazes. 'You're lucky I wasn't going any faster.'

Maggie nods and looks down the street. Harold Bray has long gone.

'Where were you heading in such a rush?' Ivy asks. 'Gerald would have had my head if I'd squashed you.'

Feeling a bit embarrassed, Maggie tells her why she had been riding so frantically.

Ivy grins. 'I think I would have done the same thing if I were you. That young chap Bray is a legend in the making.'

Maggie tells Ivy about her plan for an all-girls

football match. 'But it's really hard to find players. I don't suppose you want to play with us?'

'That's a bold idea,' Ivy says. 'Imagine the looks on the men's faces, including my Fred, if they saw us playing their game. I'm with you, kid. I'd rather kick the footy than just watch the blokes play it.'

And with that, Maggie has forgotten the bruises going purple on her legs and the grazes stinging her skin. She's just found her next player.

11

'Read all about it! The war steps up on our doorstep. High alert in Java as defenders ready themselves for Japanese attack!' Gerald bellows at the top of his lungs. 'Read all about it in your Saturday morning edition of the *Argus*!'

Maggie crosses Fitzroy Street, enters the St Kilda train station and walks up to join Gerald on the platform.

'That's right, ladies and gentlemen, Java! That's just north of this fine country. Allied planes are bombing our enemies in occupied Sumatra. Will they prevail? Read all about it!' he shouts as passengers hop off a train that's just come in from the city.

People pass Gerald coins and he hands out newspaper after newspaper as the crowd passes him.

Maggie loves that Gerald enjoys his part-time job

as a newsboy. He revels in how theatrical it is, calling out the news to passersby, trying to make it exciting enough that they'll buy a newspaper from him. His powerful voice echoes throughout the station and he sells more papers than the other newspaper boys competing for his spot.

A red Tait train rattles into the station, its brakes hissing and then screeching loudly to a stop.

Maggie thinks about the pilots battling the Japanese over the Pacific Ocean, and wonders if that will be Patrick soon – flying over the islands north of Australia, trying to drive the enemy out and stop them from advancing closer to home.

'Step right up! Step right up! Get your news, folks! Get the *Argus* here!'

Gerald's leather money satchel is slung over his right shoulder and a belt that's wrapped around a stack of newspapers hangs on his other shoulder.

Maggie taps him on the back.

'I only have a few more to sell, then we can go,' he says.

As Maggie steps aside for Gerald to finish up, she spots Gorgeous George.

'Hi, George,' she calls out, trying not to blush.

'Hello, Maggie,' he says. 'Where are you off to?'

'I'm just waiting for Gerald and then we're off to

the pictures,' Maggie says, feeling her cheeks go even redder as she catches Gerald laughing at her. 'Where are you going?'

'Oh, nowhere,' he says. 'I'm fifteen now so I need to start thinking about what to do when I leave school. I was here about a job – they're looking for a station-master's assistant.'

He waves, and Maggie sighs as she watches him exit the platform.

But the image of Mickey Mulligan swaggering into the station ruins her view.

'Hey, Fitzgerald, this is a job for news*boys*, not news*girls*!' he says. 'I bet you haven't made as much as me.'

Mickey also sell newspapers, but at one of the plum positions in the city – right outside Flinders Street Station. He's bullied the other newsies away from the spot and he's tough enough to keep even the older newsboys from stealing it.

'Keep moving, Mickey,' Maggie snaps at him.

'Or what?'

'Or I'll tackle you to the ground again. In front of everyone.'

'I dare you,' Mickey snarls. 'Although going by the scratches and bruises on you, you've already been tackled.'

72

'Good morning, Mickey,' Gerald cuts in, trying to defuse the situation. 'You won't believe what happened. Maggie saw Harold Bray yesterday. And she nearly got to chat to him. Well, almost. Isn't that great?'

'She just makes things up,' Mickey scoffs. 'Like that spy plane. She lives in a fantasy world. That's why she thinks sheilas can play footy.'

Mickey reaches forward and snatches Gerald's money bag off him.

'No! Give it back!' Gerald cries.

Mickey laughs, swinging the satchel above his head.

Maggie lunges after him, but he sidesteps her, still laughing as if it's one big joke. But Maggie doesn't give up and goes after him again. She chases him, running, dodging, darting around annoyed weekend commuters. 'Stop, thief!' she yells.

Then someone steps out from behind one of the platform signposts and bumps Mickey right off his feet. It's a serious hip-and-shoulder.

He lands hard and drops the satchel as he hits the ground.

Maggie grabs the money bag and turns to thank the person who's helped out.

It's Elena!

Mickey wobbles back up onto his feet, stunned to see that it's Elena who's taken him out.

Maggie is gobsmacked too. 'That was brilliant!' she gasps.

Elena shrugs. 'Us country kids are tougher than you might think. And I don't like thieves.'

Mickey is fuming. He clenches his fist, his face flushed. He's clearly embarrassed.

Gerald runs up to Elena and Maggie. 'Thanks, girls! Now that was jolly good to see.' He grins, taking his money bag back.

'You're going to pay for that,' Mickey growls through clenched teeth, brushing himself off. 'I'll give all three of you a good hiding. As for you, Maggie Flanagan, I don't know why anyone would want to be seen with a rotten traitor and a poncy show-pony. A right couple of no-good peculiars!'

'You take that back,' Maggie snaps.

'No, I won't,' Mickey snorts, shoving Maggie.

Maggie shoves him back, but at that moment a familiar figure steps in between them. It's Maggie's dad.

'Mickey Mulligan, you lay a finger on my girl or Gerald, and I'll give you a swift kick up the backside. In fact, go near them again and I'll kick you from here to Timbuktu,' he says, towering over Mickey. 'And don't think I won't be having a few words with your old man next time I see him. Now get out of here.'

Mickey scowls at Maggie, Elena and Gerald, before he turns and runs away.

'Dad, what are you doing here?' Maggie asks.

'Just finished up at Flinders Street, now I'm working on the clocks here,' he says. 'Who's your new friend?'

Maggie introduces Elena.

'Spinelli?' Mr Flanagan says, startled. 'Italian?'

'I'm Australian!' Elena snaps defensively. 'And my mother's Australian. So is my aunty. I live with her. I'm not doing anything wrong.'

'Dad . . .' Maggie cuts in. 'Please, don't.'

She hopes her dad won't say anything to upset Elena when she's only just started to talk to them.

'I'm sorry, Elena,' says Maggie's dad. 'I'm just surprised. I had a Swiss-Italian chap work for me, Bert D'Amico. He'd never even lived in Italy, only in Switzerland. He's no spy. But as soon as the Italians sided with the Germans . . . well, people like Bert and his family didn't have a chance. He was dragged away a couple of months ago and put in an internment camp.'

Maggie looks to Elena. She looks pale and upset, like she might cry, and her fists are clenched by her sides.

'I didn't mean to upset you, love,' says Maggie's dad, noticing the look on Elena's face. 'It's a bit harsh, I reckon, but they're just trying to protect Queen and country, right? Like it or not, Italy is our enemy now. I better get back to work. You kids, try to keep out of trouble.'

'Is that why you came to live with your aunt? Has your dad been sent to a camp?' Gerald asks when Maggie's dad has left.

Elena nods. 'My mother needs my brothers' help on our farm, but she's sent me to stay with my aunt so I can keep going to school. Mum thought it might be better in the city, but it's not.'

'I don't get it,' says Maggie. 'What's an internment camp?'

Elena sighs heavily. 'It's like a prison, but Dad hasn't done anything wrong. He's been here most of his life. He's an Australian, just like your dads are. Now he's seen as a traitor. People in town started calling him an "enemy alien". Then some men in uniforms showed up and took him away.'

Maggie looks at the ground, finding it hard to put together the right words.

But as usual, Gerald seems to know just what to say.

'I'm so sorry, Elena,' he says. 'Thank you for being

a no-good peculiar person with me. It's nice to have the company.'

Elena smiles. It's the first time Maggie has ever seen her face light up.

'You're welcome. We have to look out for each other,' she says. 'I wanted to tell you the other day that you have a beautiful singing voice.'

Gerald tips his cap at her. 'You should see my tap dancing.' He breaks into a step-ball-change. 'I taught myself from watching so many musical pictures. We're off to the Astor now to see a film, if you'd like to join us.'

It's a bit funny watching her best friend get on so well with someone else, and Maggie starts to feel slightly left out, but she tells herself not to be silly.

'Thanks, but I'm heading into the city,' Elena says. 'When my aunt finishes her shift at work, we're going to take a walk through the Botanical Gardens. See you at school, Gerald. Bye, Maggie.'

'All right. Let's go, or we'll be late,' says Gerald.

Maggie turns and waves to her father, who's up on a ladder winding one of the clocks hanging above the station's main platform. He waves back, and Maggie runs after Gerald.

12

Maggie is always amazed by the Astor's brightly lit foyer, the stained-glass windows and the bold swirl-patterned carpets. But it's the coming-attraction boards framed in stars that make Gerald giddy with excitement.

'Did you know this was called the Lyceum Theatre and then the State Theatre?' says Gerald. 'But it was never as glorious as this. Imagine when the pictures didn't have any sound! Sound is the best bit. Just imagine not being able to hear the actors sing.' He hands some coins to Maggie. 'Here's a bob for the lolly bar.'

Maggie smiles at how happy he is. 'Why are you giving me money? Aren't you supposed to be helping your mum and nan with your pay?'

'Yes. But today this is on me,' Gerald says, stepping

up to the ticket booth. 'I made some great tips in the last couple of weeks. I think I'm allowed to spoil myself once in a while – and that includes spoiling my best friend.'

'Did your nan talk your mum into letting you go to the pictures?' Maggie says.

Gerald laughs. 'Yes, she did! So enjoy it!'

They pay sixpence each for entry. Gerald grabs Maggie's arm and pulls her over to the bar.

'Gerald! It's too much!' gasps Maggie.

But Gerald just shushes her and they hand over threepence each for an ice-cream wafer, and another threepence each for a big bag of lollies that includes musk sticks, chocolate-coated orange Jaffas, aniseed balls and rosy apple lollipops.

When they reach the second-level foyer, they are so busy gabbing that they almost don't notice when an usherette, dressed in a tangerine-and-green uniform, asks for their tickets.

Maggie sighs happily as she chews on a Jaffa.

'This is the most magical place to be on a Saturday afternoon,' says Gerald, taking his ticket stub back from the usherette.

'I don't want to rain on your parade, Gerald,' says Maggie. 'But the most magical place to be on a Saturday afternoon is the MCG. I'm over summer now and I can't wait for the footy to start.'

'I hear you,' the usherette cuts in. 'Give me the Melbourne Cricket Ground any day. We'd better have footy this season. I'm sick of the war ruining everything.'

The usherette, who looks a bit younger than Rita, leads Maggie and Gerald to their dress-circle seats.

'What now?' Gerald asks, noticing a strange expression on Maggie's face.

'Hold these,' she says, handing Gerald her lollies and ice-cream wafer and running back to the foyer.

Several minutes later, Maggie returns to her seat grinning from ear to ear.

'So?' Gerald asks. 'What was all that about?'

'I found another player,' Maggie whispers excitedly. 'Her name's Annette. She *loves* footy. And she would love to play! That makes it me, Nancy, Marian, Ivy, and now Annette.'

Gerald shakes his head. 'You're absolutely crackers. They'll never let you.'

'It's not crackers to want to do what you love,' Maggie says. 'Imagine if people said you couldn't do what you love just because you're a boy.'

Gerald laughs. 'Singing and dancing? They say that all the time.'

Suddenly the theatre darkens, the curtain pulls

back, and the audience applauds. The giant screen glows brightly and a newsreel flickers to life.

'But, look!' Maggie whispers. 'We're about to see a film full of Hollywood stars. And most of them are men. You can look up to them. Girls never get to see girls playing footy. Who do *we* get to look up to?'

Maggie and Gerald are quiet for the newsreel before the show. The British-sounding announcer reads the news with dramatic music playing over black-and-white footage showing the port of Darwin demolished by the Japanese bombing attack.

Maggie doesn't know anyone who's ever been to Darwin, but she imagines the fear when they realised they were caught off-guard – the running and hiding and then coming back to see the damage.

She stops chewing on her lollies as she watches the reel project images of planes with the red sun symbol just like the one she saw. Maggie thinks of her brother Patrick again. Is he defending or attacking? Or both? She shudders. Is he dropping bombs on towns like Darwin in Europe? Or is he being shot down?

As the announcer concludes his report, Maggie's mind goes back to the enemy plane. What if it comes back and catches *us* off guard – and we're all blown to smithereens in this picture theatre? The thought makes Maggie shiver.

The movie begins, and all the singing, dancing and the magic of Oz help Maggie forget about the war for a little while. She smiles as she watches Gerald silently sing along to all the grand musical sequences.

Towards the end of the film, she stretches and starts looking at the people in the rows around her, their faces all aglow from the flickering screen.

She catches sight of a familiar face a few rows back.

It's Rita! She's leaning into a man who has his arm around her. He's a handsome American soldier, in a full starched and pressed uniform.

Maggie nudges Gerald and gestures to the rear of the theatre.

'Crikey!' Gerald whispers. 'Your sister's canoodling with a Yank!'

So that explains who she was with the other night, thinks Maggie. Wait until Dad hears about this . . .

Suddenly something occurs to Maggie, something that might work in her favour.

When the movie ends, everyone streams out of the theatre and onto the street. Maggie and Gerald wind their way through the crowd to catch up with Rita and her American date.

'So . . . fancy seeing you here,' Maggie says, tapping her sister on the shoulder.

Rita turns, startled. She takes a step away from her date.

'What are you two doing here?'

Gerald bursts into *Over the Rainbow*, one of the songs from the movie, complete with a spin and bow.

'Not now, Gerald!' Rita snaps.

'We just watched the same picture.' Maggie grins. 'Actually, you were only a few rows behind us.'

Clearly embarrassed, Rita introduces the good-looking American soldier as Henry.

'So nice to meet you, Maggie,' Henry says, smiling broadly. 'I can see the resemblance – both Australian beauties, antipodean rays of sunshine.'

Maggie pulls a face.

'I better get back to base, kids,' Henry adds. 'Sweetheart, I'll catch you later.'

Maggie grimaces again as Henry leans in and kisses her sister. Gerald elbows Maggie in the ribs.

As soon as he's out of earshot, Rita whips round to Maggie. 'You know, sometimes you can be a right little –'

'Oh, dear. What's Terry going to think?' Maggie asks, raising her eyebrows. 'You know . . . your boyfriend.'

'I told you. Terry is not my boyfriend!'

'Well, I don't really care,' Maggie says. 'And I won't

tell Mum or Dad if you promise to ask all the women at your factory if any of them would like to play football with me on my team.'

Rita glares at Maggie for a second. 'Fine!' she huffs.

'Thank you, my antipodean ray of sunshine,' Maggie says, and laughs.

13

During lunchtime on Thursday, Maggie goes searching for Gerald.

'Oh, there you are,' she says, spotting him in the corner of the busy quadrangle laughing with Elena. 'What's so funny?'

'Oh, Elena just told a joke. What's one thing you'll never get a chicken to do?'

Maggie shrugs.

'The foxtrot!'

Elena giggles. 'You know, because foxes eat chickens! Never mind. I have to see Sister Clare so I'll see you both later.'

She jumps up and Maggie and Gerald watch her cross the quad. For the first time, she holds her head up and smiles at a few of the others.

'She's like a different person this week,' says Maggie.

But then Mickey shouts at her. 'Oi, Elena,' he yells. 'Where are your Nazi mates?'

His friend Jimmy joins in. 'Watch your backs. Traitor coming through.'

A few of the kids laugh.

Maggie sees Elena's head go down again. Her shoulders hunch over.

'Sod off, pea brains!' Maggie shouts at the boys, but it doesn't seem to cheer Elena up at all. She just walks more quickly to get out of the quadrangle.

'Maggie, such language! I might have to report you,' says Frances, promenading past as if she's in a royal procession.

Maggie sticks her tongue out as she pulls Gerald away and heads inside the door to the main office. She sneaks down the hall, beckoning Gerald to follow her.

'What are we doing here?' whispers Gerald, as they huddle behind a bookcase in the corridor. 'That's Sister Gertrude's office. This is a bad idea!'

Maggie shushes him, as Sister Gertrude marches through the door and off down the hall.

And then Maggie makes her move. She slips through the open door and into the principal's office.

'Do you want to get the cane again or are you just completely mad?' Gerald whispers, following Maggie in. 'I don't want the cane. What are you doing?'

'I've got to pray,' says Maggie, looking up to the portrait of Jesus' mum. 'And I want you to keep a lookout.'

'Here? Why not in the church? Or at home, or kneeling by your bed like normal people?' says Gerald nervously, standing in the doorway, glancing back over his shoulder. 'If Sister Gertrude catches us, who knows what she'll do.'

'Dear Mary, Mother of God,' Maggie addresses the painting. 'It's all right that I got the cane. I won't hold that against you. And, actually, I did come up with quite a clever plan. But thank you for helping me find the players I've found so far. I really do need more to come forward, though. So . . . um, if it's all right, I'm asking if you could please help with that. And also look after Pat. Thank you for your time. A-women.'

'A-women?' says Gerald, relieved that Maggie is already leaving the office and is making her way back towards the quad. He hurries after her. 'What was all that about?'

Maggie fills him in. 'That's why I've been so lucky finding players,' she says. 'It's sort of a miracle.'

Gerald looks dubious. 'Really, Maggie? That seems unlikely. I mean, she probably has more important prayers to answer, surely?'

'Hello, Maggie and Gerald,' Nancy says, popping out from a classroom doorway. She looks both ways, like a spy making sure no one is listening. 'Are you still thinking of the charity football match, Maggie?'

Maggie nods. 'I've been able to rope others into playing. And my sister is going to find me some more players at her work.'

'That's great.' Nancy grins. 'Some of my old team-mates are keen to play again. Five of them!'

'Five?' Maggie says loudly, then repeats it in a whisper. 'Five?'

'Yes, so keep me updated, all right?' Nancy winks, before heading back inside.

'Can you believe it? Five! All together that makes . . .' Before Maggie can finish, Gerald charges off.

'Where are you going?' Maggie calls after him.

'I'm going back to pray to that painting and ask Mary for her help. I want her to put me on stage in front of an audience!'

Maggie grins. 'I told you it was a miracle,' she says.

—

Later that day, after school, Maggie is in Gerald's backyard with plans to build him a billycart.

'Rope . . . check. Crate box . . . check. Wood and

nails and screws . . . check. Saw and screwdriver . . . check. Hammer . . . check! Strange turning metal thing and brackets that I have no idea what to do with . . . check. Now, where do we begin?' Gerald sighs. 'I don't even have wheels. I'm glad your dad could get us these billycart things, but maybe we should ask him to help us build it too.'

Maggie catches Gerald's gaze drop, his mind taken somewhere else. She can see he's thinking of his own father and brother – it's the same way she looks when she's really missing Patrick. It's a vacant stare, a moment when that yearning feeling is so strong and gripping it freezes you like a statue.

'Hello?' comes a cry from the side of the house.

'We won't have to ask my dad,' says Maggie, snapping Gerald out of it. 'We've got Nora. We're here at the back, Nora!'

Nora appears, grinning. She's holding four old wheels that look like they've come off a pram, two long thin pieces of metal and a small drill with a handle you can wind by hand.

'We were just about to get started,' says Gerald.

'Right then, pass me the saw,' Nora orders.

Maggie and Gerald watch, gobsmacked, as Nora goes about sawing and nailing and attaching.

The bits of wood and the crate look more and more

like a billycart every minute.

'Now we have to make sure that the timber front and rear axles match, you see . . .' she says. 'If I position the brackets here and cut the box here and make sure the wheels are aligned with this part . . .'

Maggie and Gerald try to help when they can, but mostly they just watch in awe.

'And there it is!' Nora announces, hopping to her feet, stepping back, proud of herself. 'Your billycart is raring to go and ready for the derby. It just needs a coat of paint, but I'll let you do that, Gerald.'

'Let's try it out!' Maggie suggests.

The three of them roll the cart out into the back lane and around to the street. Gerald is the first to ride it, with Maggie and Nora pushing him as fast as they can.

'Faster!' Gerald hollers. 'Faster! Faster!'

'My turn!' Maggie cries, as they run out of breath and roll to a stop. 'Too bad our street is flat. We really do need a hill.'

'I think Nora should go next,' says Gerald. 'After all, she did build it.'

Maggie agrees, and she and Gerald push Nora as if they're running for their lives. They make it all the way down their street and come to a screeching stop right in front of Miss Kelly's Corner Store, laughing and talking over each other excitedly.

'Oh, I wish I was allowed to race in the derby.' Nora sighs, hopping out of the cart to let Maggie have a go.

'Not in a million years would Sister Gertrude allow you to do that, otherwise I'd happily let you take my spot,' Gerald says.

'You've just given me a great idea,' says Maggie. 'But, Nora, if you like my idea, I was wondering, would you play football for my charity match in return?'

Nora nods and Maggie shares her plan. She calls it the Great Derby Secret Mission.

'So are we all in agreement?' Maggie concludes.

'For sure,' says Gerald. 'I can't believe we're going to do this.'

'It's genius, Maggie. It's a deal,' says Nora, shaking Maggie's hand, just as Frances steps out from the store.

'What's going on here? What are you doing here with them?' she snaps, startling Nora.

'Um, I just bumped into them,' Nora lies. 'What are you doing?'

'I needed a new hairbrush,' Frances says, staring at them suspiciously. 'Why don't you come to my place, Nora, and we can do each other's hair.'

'Um, sure,' Nora says, walking after Frances, who has already marched off.

Nora looks back over her shoulder and grins at Maggie and Gerald.

Maggie gives her a thumbs-up.

'All right, get in, and I'll push you back,' says Gerald, turning the billycart around.

'Hold on a few minutes,' she replies. 'While I'm here I'm going to the store. There's something I need.'

14

Miss Kelly's Corner Store sells everything from matches to lollies to cereal to cans of beans to bars of soap. Maggie notices today's newspaper headlines displayed on the stand: *Batavia, Dutch East Indies falls – Japanese move in!* Maggie exhales. The enemy is picking up momentum.

What would Melbourne be like if we were invaded? she thinks, but quickly tries not to imagine such a horrible thought.

Miss Kelly, the owner of the store, is on a small ladder packing away some biscuits.

'Be with you in just a sec,' she says, her back to Maggie.

'That's all right,' says Maggie, wandering over to the magazine and book stand.

She browses through the latest *Women's Weekly*

magazine and then looks through the collection of books.

'So, Maggie,' says Miss Kelly. 'Are you after something to read?'

Miss Kelly is around the same age as Maggie's mother. She's not married and has no family. Everyone in the neighbourhood likes her, but Maggie knows that other people call her a 'spinster'. Maggie's not sure what it means, but they never say it to her face.

'It's a shame and very sad,' Maggie once overheard her mum say to Rita.

Maggie didn't know what that meant either. Why do adults always think it's a shame not to be married? Maggie feels sure her sister will get married, but she wonders if she ever will. For a second, she imagines herself and George walking down the aisle together, but she shrugs the thought off. She knows he's nice to her because she's Patrick's little sister.

Miss Kelly never seems sad. In fact, she always seems happy. And she spends most of her time with her best friend, Lizzie, anyway. They even share a house together.

'It's only a small collection,' Miss Kelly says, smiling. 'Is there a particular book you're looking for?'

'Do you have *Anne of Green Gables*?' asks Maggie.

'Now that *is* popular,' says Miss Kelly. 'So unfortunately, I don't have it in stock. I do have my own copy, though, and you're more than welcome to borrow it.'

Miss Kelly ducks out back and returns with the book.

'Thank you so much,' Maggie says. 'I'll return it as soon as possible.'

Miss Kelly asks Maggie if she needs anything else.

'Um, I was wondering . . . would it be possible for me to put up a notice in the shop window?'

'What sort of notice?'

Maggie hesitates, unsure whether she should tell Miss Kelly about the football match.

'Hmm, by the look of your expression, this must be a very serious notice, or perhaps you're not sure if you should put it up.' Miss Kelly smiles. 'Go on, love, you can tell me. What is it?'

Maggie takes a deep breath and tells her. But she needn't have worried. Miss Kelly's face lights up. She goes out back again and returns a few seconds later with an old newspaper. It's so old that it's dusty and yellow.

Miss Kelly opens it up and puts it down on the counter in front of Maggie.

'It's from nineteen fifteen,' she says.

Maggie can't believe her eyes. It's an article about

a group of women in Western Australia playing football. The accompanying photograph shows a blurry black-and-white image of women in full-length silk dresses and big hats, and they're chasing after a football.

'That woman there in the front trying to grab the footy is my mother,' Miss Kelly adds. 'She played for a team of shop girls against women who worked at a factory. I was about your age and I remember every minute of it! It was incredible. I was so proud of her. They raised money for our boys during the Great War. Just as you're trying to do today. I can't believe it!'

'You can't believe it?' Maggie cries. 'This is wonderful!'

'I wish I could offer to join your team,' Miss Kelly says. 'But my back would give out for sure. I'll ask Lizzie. She loves the game and she might ask her workmates too. She works at the ammunition factory in Footscray. So let's get writing that notice, eh? We'll need a date and time for the game but, first, what about a training session – where and when?'

Maggie's mind whirls. Not once has she considered training sessions, or times and dates. It was always just about the game, finding players to field two sides. She hadn't thought beyond that.

'No?' Miss Kelly says. 'Right, let me help you then. We need to find a quiet time when we can have an oval or a park to ourselves. A time when there are few people around and it won't cause too much of a stir. Can you imagine what the boys will say if a bunch of us show up and start kicking a footy alongside them?'

Maggie raises her eyebrows and smirks. 'I don't think they would be very polite,' she says.

'A lot of the girls on your team will work during the day or look after babies, and then they shop for groceries, clean the house, do the laundry and feed and look after their family, too,' Miss Kelly says. 'So the challenge is to find a time that they can all make.'

'I know!' Maggie cries. 'What about this Sunday?' Then she hesitates. Ball games, any sort of games, aren't allowed to be played on Sundays. 'But it's the day of the Lord, a rest day . . . so maybe we shouldn't.'

Maggie watches Miss Kelly thinking. Her mouth curls to a smile, and she slowly nods. Maybe the suggestion isn't such a bad idea after all.

'If we make it after Mass and after Sunday lunch, sometime mid-afternoon, we might just get away with it. There won't be anyone else at the park, that's for sure. All right, then . . . let's give it a try! Elsternwick Park, this Sunday afternoon at two o'clock.'

When Maggie leaves Miss Kelly's store, she's talking so fast that Gerald can hardly understand her.

She smiles all the way home.

Her dream of playing football just became a little more real.

15

The following morning Maggie makes sure to catch up with Marian on her milk run. She tells her about the first training session.

'I'll be there with bells on,' Marian says, swapping over the empty milk bottles by the fence with full ones. 'How exciting!'

At school, Maggie passes on the news to Nancy.

'I can't wait to tell my friends,' she says. 'I wrote to my husband telling him all about it. He's been sent over to New Guinea. Oh, I can't believe I'm going to get to do this again!'

After school, Maggie takes a detour on the way home and drops by the Astor Theatre, where she leaves a note for Annette with details about the training session.

When she finally gets home, Maggie is thrilled to

see that Ivy has just delivered ice to her house.

'Just the person I wanted to see!' Maggie calls out to her.

'G'day, Maggie,' Ivy cries.

It still feels like an odd thing for Maggie to see a woman driving a car, let alone a truck.

Ivy laughs as she walks back to talk to Maggie. 'I see you gawking at me driving the lorry. Don't be so surprised about women driving. Haven't you heard of Jean Robertson and Kathleen Howell?'

Maggie shakes her head.

Ivy's face lights up as she tells the story. 'Back in the twenties, they were the first women to drive across Australia. And then again in nineteen thirty they drove a car all the way to England, via Darwin, Malaysia, India, Syria and Egypt. No one can tell me driving or farming or welding is just for men. And you can add footy to that list too. How did you go with organising your game?'

Maggie fills her in.

'That's the way! Good on ya!' Ivy grins. 'If you get this game up, we'll show the fellas a thing or two.'

Maggie mirrors her smile.

'To tell you the truth, in the long run this war might turn out to be a good thing for us girls.'

Maggie furrows her brow. She's never heard anyone say that the war is a good thing before.

'I don't mean that I'm happy there's a war on,' Ivy continues. 'My Fred's over there and that's just awful. But it's showing that we sheilas can do anything the chaps can. Better than them in some cases, even though they pay us next to nothing compared to the men. I have two boys to raise, but if I could have it my way I'd keep doing this job even after the war ends. Keep up the good work, Maggie. See you at training.'

Ivy slams the truck door shut, starts and revs the engine, beeps the horn and drives away, leaving Maggie to imagine what it would be like to finish school and choose any of the jobs that the boys could choose.

Could she really drive a car or become a welder, or a football coach or even a pilot like Patrick? Was that really possible?

—

Later that evening, while her parents are once again gathered around the wireless, and Rita is out on another secret date with Henry the handsome American soldier, Maggie sits on the back step of her house and finishes her latest letter to Patrick.

She tells him everything. About the footy, about

seeing Harold Bray, about Elena at school, about Ivy and all the things she said about girls being able to do anything just as well as the chaps. She wonders how he will feel about that bit.

Maggie scribbles some more as the sun dips and the temperature drops. For the first time in months she feels like slipping on a cardigan. It's early March and autumn is in the air.

She can hear Gerald singing to his mum's accompaniment on the piano. Maggie looks back to her writing pad.

. . . so I borrowed Anne of Green Gables *and will probably start reading it tonight.*

Anyway, that's the news from here. Mum, Dad, Colleen (you should see how much she's grown) and I miss you terribly. Even Rita does, though she would never admit it! Be safe. Write when you can.

Your loving sister,

Carrots

Maggie puts down her letter, picks up Patrick's football and kicks it towards the back of the yard. She still has time left to get a few drills in before it gets too dark.

'And here she comes . . . the unstoppable Flying

Flanagan, bursting through the pack,' Maggie commentates, scooping the footy, pretending to baulk and weave. 'And she passes it off to her teammate, Danny the Dunny . . .'

Maggie handballs the footy against the door of the outhouse toilet – it ricochets back into her hands.

'. . . who gets it back to Flanagan . . . and she thumps it on with all her might . . .'

Maggie boots the football and it soars over the fence and into Grumpy Gaffney's backyard.

Again!

'Aw, bugger,' Maggie mutters under her breath.

By the time she climbs to the top of the fence, Grumpy Gaffney has already grabbed the ball.

'Sorry!' Maggie cries. 'Hey! Where are you going with my football?'

'I warned you,' Grumpy Gaffney growls. 'Next time you kicked it into my yard, I told you what I'd do.'

'You can't!' Maggie protests. 'Please, don't!'

But Grumpy Gaffney has already slammed the door shut behind him.

Maggie charges down alongside her house and around to Grumpy Gaffney's front door – and knocks on it loudly.

No answer.

She knocks again. And again. She can't let him

ruin Patrick's footy. Still her mean old neighbour doesn't answer.

Maggie rushes to her parents.

'Well, he did warn you,' says Maggie's mother. 'And what have I told you about playing football? It's not very ladylike, Maggie. Perhaps this is a sign to give it up. If you like sport so much, why not try hockey or netball?'

Maggie shakes her head.

'Try again in the morning. Let him cool off,' Maggie's father adds. 'I'm sure he won't puncture it. His bark is worse than his bite. He's not a bad old bloke really. He's just had a tough life. He's probably gone to bed – as you should now. Go read your book for a while.'

Feeling miserable, Maggie turns in for the evening and reads a few chapters of *Anne of Green Gables* by the dim light of the lamp. Without Patrick's footy, she has a hard time falling asleep.

First thing in the morning she knocks again at Grumpy Gaffney's door. And again, no answer.

'Right, if he's not going to give it back to me, then I'm going in to get it myself,' Maggie mumbles. 'Pat told me to look after it. So that's what I'm going to do.'

Maggie tiptoes alongside Grumpy Gaffney's house and stops just as she reaches the backyard. She peeks into the garden. Mr Gaffney's vegetable patch is near the back porch, and his bunker is at the far end of the yard. Maggie waits patiently for him to come out to tend his vegetables.

Her stomach churns. She knows what she's planning to do is wrong. Sneaking into someone's house is sure to get her into colossal trouble.

'But why does he have to be so mean?' she says under her breath.

Awash with frustration and shame, she waits. And waits. Until Grumpy Gaffney finally steps outside with his cup of tea.

Maggie makes her move and sneaks inside the back door. She tiptoes into the kitchen.

'Now where would he have put it?' she whispers.

She's never been inside Grumpy Gaffney's house before. The simple kitchen is spick and span. Nothing is out of place.

Maggie's mouth is dry and her heart is beating so fast it feels as if it's going to beat right out of her chest.

What will I do if he catches me? What if the front door is locked? What if he's already punctured it? Once he knows it's missing, he'll know I've taken it.

Maggie's mind is spinning.

When she walks into the lounge room, she spots the ball straightaway – placed right there on Grumpy Gaffney's armchair, next to the wireless.

Maggie sighs, relieved. It's still inflated. Her dad was right. The old codger *didn't* puncture it!

She goes to grab it, but leaning forward she catches sight of a framed photograph up on the wall. It shows a football team wearing guernseys with the map of Australia.

Under the image is a caption identifying the squad as the Third Australian Divisional Team, 1916. And in the frame, alongside the photograph, is a faded newspaper article. The headline causes Maggie to catch her breath.

Australian Football at Queens' Club, London.
Exhibition Game by Anzacs Draws Large Crowd.

'I don't believe it,' Maggie whispers. 'He doesn't hate footy. He loves it . . . or at least he used to.'

Maggie is so intrigued, she inches forward to take a closer look at the article and momentarily forgets where she is.

'What is the meaning of this?' Grumpy Gaffney's angry voice bellows.

16

'Get out!' Grumpy Gaffney snaps. 'Get out! How dare you? You disrespectful little girl! Wait until your parents hear about this.'

'I'm s-sorry,' Maggie stammers. 'Please, I know I shouldn't be here. I know you warned me not to kick the footy into your yard. But, please, Mr Gaffney, I just couldn't bear the thought of you puncturing Patrick's football. I didn't sleep a wink last night.'

'None of that gives you the right to come into my place, willy nilly, and make yourself at home. I have a good mind to call the law on you.'

Maggie tries her hardest not to let the sting in her eyes turn to tears. But she feels her cheeks flush and heat up like coals in a fire, and her bottom lip quiver uncontrollably.

She tells herself to be tough and not to let her

emotions get the better of her. But she can't help it. Tears start streaming down her face.

'I'm sorry. I'm sorry,' she says, sobbing and wiping her nose with the back of her hand. 'You can call the police, but this football is the one thing that reminds me of Patrick. It makes me feel close to him – even though I know he's on the other side of the world. He's with me every time I mark it or handball or kick it. I miss him so much, and I'm so afraid for him.'

Mr Gaffney's furrowed brow softens. He sighs heavily.

'Here,' Maggie says, handing the football to him. 'I'll leave now.'

'Wait,' Mr Gaffney says. The old man limps to his armchair and falls into it, rubbing his eyes as if he might cry too.

'You're right to be afraid,' he says finally. 'I fear for Patrick too, Maggie. I fear for all the boys. And for us all. I know what war can do. I've seen it up close . . . and it's not honourable or exciting. It's devasting. It's soul-crushing.'

Maggie gulps and wipes away her tears.

'To be honest,' says Grumpy Gaffney, 'I'm more afraid than I've ever been. The enemy is at our front gate, and they must not get inside.'

'I'm sorry I've upset you,' Maggie says. 'And I'm

sorry for always kicking the football into your yard.'

Grumpy Gaffney nods.

'You could always kick it back. We could kick-to-kick over the fence,' Maggie adds hopefully.

Mr Gaffney's bushy eyebrows close in together. Maggie wonders whether she's said too much, but he doesn't seem angry.

'I didn't know you played football.' She points to the photograph on the wall. 'Who were the Third Australian Divisional team?'

There's another long pause.

'They were the greatest mates any man could ever have,' Grumpy Gaffney says. 'They were a part of the infantry division of the Australian Army, and the other team, the Australian Units Training team, were also very fine servicemen.'

Maggie sits on the floor and places her footy between her crossed legs.

'Go on,' she says. 'Can you tell me? Please?'

Grumpy Gaffney nods.

'It was an exhibition match to aid the British and French Red Cross. A big crowd had showed up to watch us, including King Edward – well, he was Prince of Wales back then. The Brits seemed a bit baffled and amused by the game, but I think they were impressed by how fast-moving it all was. Many of the players were senior footy champs. I was one of only a few who hadn't played in the big leagues. Our team captain was South Melbourne's Bruce Sloss. And we also had Bill Sewart from Essendon, Dan Minogue from Collingwood, and Les Lee and Hugh James from Richmond.'

'Any St Kilda players?' asks Maggie.

'Yeah, there was Harry Moyes and Percy Jory. And the other side had their fair share of legends – Jack Cooper, Ossy Armstrong, Percy Trotter and Alf Jackson.'

Maggie watches Grumpy Gaffney's gaze turn inward. He's there now, she thinks. Back in 1916, playing alongside his mates.

He smiles and then winces. Maggie remains quiet until he snaps out of it.

He exhales. 'That's in the past now. Most of them are dead. It turned out to be the last game of footy they would ever play. A couple of months after that most of us were in the trenches.'

Maggie thinks of her dad's trench foot and her mother praying aloud in the kitchen when she doesn't think anyone is around. Maggie knows she's praying for the uncle that Maggie never knew, who died in the trenches of the Great War.

'That's awful that football reminds you of something painful,' says Maggie softly. 'But during the game, you loved it, right?'

Grumpy Gaffney nods.

'Whenever I'm really missing Patrick and I'm scared for him and for us and my stomach is full of knots, I think about us kicking the footy around, and then I feel a whole lot better. I guess that's why I'm in the middle of organising my own football match.'

'You are?' Grumpy Gaffney says, looking up.

'Yeah, an all-female football match.'

'You're not?' Grumpy Gaffney says, half-smiling.

'I am!' Maggie says proudly. 'And we have our first training session tomorrow afternoon at Elsternwick Park. I don't have enough players yet to field two sides, but I'm praying to Mary that we'll have enough soon. And we're going to play our guts out to raise money for all the boys fighting for us.'

For the first time, Maggie sees her neighbour properly smile.

'You are a stubborn, and extremely annoying young lady, but I really do believe that once you put your mind to something you are unstoppable,' he says. 'Now leave me alone – and take your footy with you.'

17

After dinner, Maggie tries to read more *Anne of Green Gables* on her bed, but is distracted by Rita fussing with her hair and makeup.

'Are you going dancing with your American soldier?' Maggie asks. 'Handsome Henry?'

'Shush!' Rita snaps. 'Keep your voice down. I don't want Mum or Dad to find out. As far as they're concerned, I'm going out with the girls. And, yes, we're going dancing.'

'To the opening of that new dance hall?'

'Yes, it's a club for servicemen on Swanston Street in the city. All the Americans go there.' Rita slips into her best navy-blue A-line dress. She straightens the small white collar. 'Well, how do I look?'

Maggie hates to admit it, but her big sister looks beautiful and like a proper grown-up.

'You scrub up all right,' she says.

'I'll take that as a compliment. Right, I better go, or I'll be late.'

'Rita?' Maggie says as she starts to close the bedroom door. 'Did you ask your friends at work if they would like to play football? Because tomorrow we have our first training . . .'

But Rita's not listening. Before Maggie can get another word out, she's through the front door.

'Maggie!' their mother cries from the kitchen. 'Can you duck next door and ask the Fitzgeralds if they could spare us some milk?'

Gerald answers the door when she knocks.

Maggie blinks. He's wearing a dress and has ribbons in his curly hair.

'Um . . . should I even ask?' Maggie says. 'Are you wearing rouge?'

'Just a touch! You've just missed my lounge room concert for Nan and Mum,' he says. 'Can you guess who I am?'

Maggie shakes her head.

Gerald bursts into song.

'On the Good Ship Lollipop . . .'

Maggie shrugs. 'It's familiar, but I can't place it.'

'Come on, Maggie. It's obvious! I'm Shirley Temple! That's her signature song!' Gerald says, waving Maggie inside.

'Oh, of course you are. You're the spitting image of a world-famous, all-singing, all-dancing Hollywood star!' She laughs. 'Well, Shirley, could I borrow some milk, please?'

'Oh, hello, Maggie,' says Gerald's mother. 'You've just missed Gerald's concert. He does a great Shirley.'

'What was that, dear?' Nan Fitzgerald asks, her hearing as bad as ever. 'Who does what?'

'I was just saying to Maggie, Mother, that Gerald does a great Shirley,' repeats Gerald's mum, raising her voice.

'Oh, yes, I know Gerald *is* girly, but we love him just the way he is,' Nan says.

'No, Mum. I said *Shirley*, not girly. Oh, never mind!'

Mrs Fitzgerald tells Maggie that she'll take a cup of milk over to Maggie's mum herself. She's been wanting to catch up with her. 'You two have fun at the working bee at school tonight,' she adds. 'I'm glad that the Sisters have arranged some of the parents to chaperone you home when you're done.'

Maggie throws a baffled look at Gerald.

'What working bee? What's going on?' she whispers.

Gerald shushes her until his mother steps out through the front door and is out of earshot.

'I just made that up,' Gerald exclaims. 'I told her that I'd volunteered to help the Sisters paint the new picket fence around the convent's garden, but I'm really going out to meet Elena. We've arranged to meet in the city – and there's no way my mother will let me do that.'

'What? Are you going now?'

'Yes, there's still plenty of light out thanks to that whole saving-daylight thing.'

Maggie knows Gerald is referring to Daylight Saving time. It was introduced only a couple months ago to save energy during the war. It's light until late, so that means more time for her to be outside, kicking the football in the backyard.

'Elena's aunt just got an extra job clearing tables at a new dance hall,' Gerald tells her. 'It's the opening night, tonight. Elena said she might be able to sneak us in and we could see some top dancing and a real professional swing band. Isn't that the most smashing thing ever? And I'll finally have something to confess in church! You've gotta come with me! Go and tell your mum now, while my mother is over there. It's perfect. She'll back me up. I said you were helping out too, in case you wanted to come.'

'Um, I'm not so sure,' Maggie says. 'This is not like you at all, lying to your mum and Nan like that.

115

You're asking for some big Hail Marys. I'm not sure it's something we should be doing.'

'You mean like organising an all-girls football match when you were told not to, or crash tackling Mickey Mulligan?' Gerald laughs. 'Come on, Maggie. This is my dream! I've seen so many dance routines on the silver screen, a chance to see them in real life, in a swanky new city dance hall would be out of this world.'

'All right, I'll come,' Maggie says. 'But aren't you forgetting one thing?' She gestures at Gerald's Shirley Temple costume.

'Oh, you're right,' Gerald says. 'Imagine me stepping out like this? Imagine Mickey catching a squiz? Just one more excuse for him to beat me up.'

'He wouldn't dare!' Maggie calls after Gerald as he ducks into his bedroom to change. 'Not if Elena and I were around!'

18

Maggie and Gerald hop off the tram at Flinders Street Station. An ant-like parade of vehicles is motoring up and down the main streets.

They run down Swanston Street, past St Paul's Cathedral, across Flinders Lane and Collins Street, and finally they reach the Capitol Theatre.

Milling in front of the ornate building is a large crowd of uniformed American and Australian servicemen and young women with their hair done, wearing their finest dresses.

Maggie and Gerald weave their way through the excited crowd. Gerald looks around frantically for Elena.

'I can't see her,' he says, standing on his tiptoes.

'Maybe she's already inside,' says Maggie. 'Let's push forward.' She shoves her way to the front of the crowd with Gerald close behind.

But when they reach the entrance of the building, they're stopped by a plump doorman in a maroon uniform.

'Hey, you two! Where do you think you're going?' he barks. 'This isn't a place for kids.'

'I'm looking for my friend Elena,' says Gerald. 'Her aunt works here. She's brunette, about this tall? Have you seen her?'

'Look around, kid,' the doorman says. 'You've just described half the women here. Now stand aside and let the adults through.'

'Gerald!' a voice calls.

It's Elena and she's with a lady who must be her aunt.

'Right, I can't let you kids in for long,' says Elena's aunt matter-of-factly. 'And I'm only doing this because I'm grateful to you, young man, for the little joy you've brought to Elena by being such a sweet friend to her.'

Elena's aunt tousles Gerald's hair.

He blushes.

Maggie starts to feel slightly on the outer – as if she's seated on the boundary while her team plays on.

'This way,' says Elena's aunt. 'Staff aren't allowed through the main entrance.'

They walk back on to Swanston Street, through the crowd, turning left into Little Collins Street, and then another left into a laneway that takes them to the back entrance of the Capitol Building. They march down some basement stairs, through a kitchen of hard-at-work cooks and cleaners, and finally through two doors and down a corridor, that eventually leads into a large ballroom.

Gerald gasps as they peek around the doorway. When they step out into the room, it's as if they've just stepped into another world.

Maggie and Gerald are swept up by the blaring swing music coming from a seventeen-piece big band on the stage. The dance floor below is packed with couples feverishly dancing under a canopy of twinkly fairy lights.

'Crikey!' Gerald says, his feet already moving, his hips already swaying to the music. 'They're doing the jitterbug! This is heaven!'

'It's wonderful,' sighs Elena. 'It's just like being in America!'

Some of the American soldiers are showing off with a new flamboyant dance style. The women looking on are dazzled, but the Aussie servicemen in the room don't look impressed.

Just as she's wondering if Handsome Henry can

dance like that, Maggie feels a hand on her shoulder. She jumps with fright.

'Maggie?' It's her sister's voice. 'What are you doing here?'

She spins around.

It is Rita. And Terry is standing by her side!

'Terry?' Maggie cries. 'But . . .'

'G'day, Maggie!' Terry smiles. 'What are you doing here? You're too young to be in a club surely?'

'She most certainly is,' says Rita, now looking annoyed. 'Terry, could you please get me a drink?'

Terry nods and makes his way to the bar.

'What about Henry?' Maggie asks, looking around to see if the American soldier is nearby.

'A lady has every right to change her mind,' Rita exclaims. 'Now what's the meaning of this? Why are you here? Do Mum and Dad know?'

'We're just here to visit Elena's aunt,' Maggie tells her, introducing Elena. 'But you know how Gerald loves music . . .'

'Where is Gerald?' Rita cuts in, sounding worried.

'He was standing here a second ago,' Elena says over the music.

Everyone looks around the crowded room. Gerald is nowhere to be seen.

The music abruptly stops. 'Ladies and Gentlemen!'

The conductor of the big band takes the mic. He's framed by a giant spotlight. 'You are in for a wonderful evening. Today we have a special treat for you. A young lad has impressed the musical director so much with a few bars of his favourite tune that we're putting him up here on stage to perform for you. It's been his dream to sing in front of an audience and his brother and father are up at Puckapunyal so he wants to give something back to the troops. Without further ado, please give it up for Gerald Fitzgerald!'

'What?' Maggie and Elena say at the same time.

Maggie can't believe it as they watch Gerald step up to the microphone. Her heart is racing for him, but he looks more relaxed and poised than she has ever seen him. He seems completely at home up there under the bright lights.

'What will he sing?' asks Elena.

Maggie's not sure. Surely, she thinks, he'll do a song from one of the upbeat Hollywood pictures he's dragged her along to see.

But Gerald takes a deep breath and begins. He's singing alone, without the band . . .

'It's *Waltzing Matilda*,' says Rita.

Then the band joins in – saxophones, trumpets and trombones.

The crowd cheers and begins to sing along.

They're singing for their loved ones.

They're singing for those they've lost.

They're singing for Australia.

Maggie raises her voice along with them. She thinks of Patrick and belts out the iconic Australian tune with pride. And when Gerald finishes his performance, the hall erupts into applause and cheers.

As the clapping dies down, Gerald makes an unexpected announcement.

'Thank you, everyone. While I'm up here, I just want to say that my best mate, Maggie, is doing her bit for the war effort too. She's trying to organise the impossible – an all-female football match to raise money for all of you fine servicemen. She's looking for players and for a paying crowd. So, ladies, please contact Miss Kelly's corner shop in East St Kilda if you're interested and, everyone else, please turn up to see the game at Elsternwick Park at two o'clock next Saturday. Thank you. And good night!'

19

Maggie walks slowly down the church aisle behind other parishioners to receive communion. She kneels at the altar rail and waits for Father Finney and Jimmy the altar boy to reach her.

Father Finney raises the communion wafer above her and says some words in Latin, to which Maggie responds 'Amen', and then quickly says under her breath, 'A-women.'

Back in her pew with her family, Maggie waits for the wafer stuck to her tongue to dissolve.

She looks around the church. Even with most of the fathers and older brothers away, it's packed.

She sees Gerald across the aisle wedged between his mum and Nan. Frances is down the front, dressed to the nines and is sitting upright, more rigid than a stop sign. Alongside her, her three older sisters are equally dressed in their best. A couple of them are holding toddlers on their hips. Nora is squeezed up against her four wriggly brothers and her mother, who is cradling a baby. Nora's mum looks dishevelled and tired as she tries to blow away a long strand of hair hanging over her eyes.

Mickey is seated beside his mother. All his older siblings are married and have families of their own. His dad isn't there. He's probably sleeping after his shift as a dunnyman.

Now there's one job I don't want, thinks Maggie. I'm happy to leave emptying out the dunnycans to the boys.

Mickey is definitely not praying. In fact, he's picking his nose. Once he notices Maggie watching him, he quickly pulls his finger out of his nostril and sticks his tongue out at her.

Maggie rolls her eyes and then notices Elena sitting with her aunt. As usual, she's slouched low in her pew, as if she's trying to shrink herself and not be seen.

Maggie waves at her, but then spots Sister Gertrude glaring from one of the pews near Elena.

Maggie quickly drops her head.

When she looks back up again, Sister Gertrude is thankfully once again facing the altar, deep in prayer beside Sister Agnes and Sister Clare.

At the end of service, Father Finney makes an announcement about the big fundraiser event planned for the following Saturday.

'I'd expect you all to support what's going to be a wonderful morning. Part of Barkly Street will be shut off so our Grade Fives and Sixes can hold their brilliant billycart derby and sewing and cake stalls. Which reminds me, I'd tell you a sewing joke, but I don't have any material. Get it? Material, comic material?' He laughs. 'Anyway, not only does it promise to be a great event, but every penny will go to our boys fighting abroad. So, please, tell all your family and friends. Peace be with you and enjoy the rest of your day.'

As everyone streams out of the church, Maggie heads for Elena. She steps away from her aunt.

'Um, I wanted to ask you last night,' Maggie says, suddenly feeling worried about how Elena will respond. 'But it was Gerald's moment and I . . .'

Maggie takes a deep breath.

'I know you said that you don't want to play football because you don't want to stand out and draw more attention to yourself, but your curly black hair and your dark eyes, the colour of your skin . . . it's you, and they're all just going to have to deal with it.'

Maggie points at the rest of the people talking in groups around them. 'I finished *Anne of Green Gables*, that book you were reading. I used to be embarrassed by my red hair too, just like in the story. Especially when Mickey and Jimmy would tease me about it. But now I don't care what they think. They'll make fun of me anyway because I don't like girly things and I want to play footy. But I'm not going to allow that to stop me.'

Elena sighs.

'I know you mean well,' she says, 'but you don't get it, do you? Having red hair and a good old Irish name that everyone can pronounce isn't so bad. You *are* brave for trying to play football, but I'd settle for being accepted as a person with all the same rights as you. I'd settle for not having to worry about being locked up one day for being myself, like my poor dad. Gerald and I might joke with each other about being the odd ones out, but deep down we're not laughing. Do you know what I just heard in there, in church? Someone whispered from the pew behind me: "Traitors should be shot!" Last week someone at school said, "Go back to where you come from," and they don't mean Murchison.'

Maggie is mortified. 'Oh, Elena, I'm so sorry,' she says. 'I feel . . . I feel silly now.'

As Elena shrugs and returns to her aunt, Sister Gertrude walks towards Maggie.

'What are you two up to?' she snaps.

'Carrots! Time to go!' Maggie's father calls.

'Nothing, Sister. Got to run. Bye now!' Maggie blurts, dashing off, her heart pounding.

She grabs hold of her father's hand and leaves the churchyard, looking back over her shoulder. As she watches Elena and her aunt walking away, she wonders what it would be like to know that your dad is locked up somewhere like a criminal, and that you might be next.

20

'What's up with you?' Maggie's mother calls from the open kitchen window. 'What are you doing pacing up and down the yard? Ever since we got back from church, you've been flittering about like a willy wagtail in spring.'

Maggie is stewing about whether to tell her parents about the football match. She's feeling guilty about sneaking off to the training session at the park.

But what if they say no? she thinks. Who am I kidding! It's a Sunday! Of course they'll say no. What if they put a stop to me doing all of this? I can't risk it. But I also don't want to lie again.

Maggie steps inside and takes a deep breath.

Just as she's preparing to tell her mum everything, Rita steps into the kitchen holding a wicker basket filled with balls of yarn.

'Maggie, I could do with some help. You'll need to come with me for the afternoon,' she says.

'Where?' Maggie and her mum ask in unison.

'I'm off to Judith's to knit scarves for the Red Cross, and we need all the help we can get. Come on, Maggie.'

'No!' Maggie says, glaring at Rita as if to say, 'What are you doing? You know I have to be somewhere else.'

Rita gives her a meaningful look. Maggie knows she can't argue, as Rita hasn't dobbed on her about sneaking out to the dance hall . . . yet!

'That's a good idea,' says their mum. 'Go with your sister.'

Maggie can't believe it. Annoyed and frustrated, she stomps out of the house and follows Rita down the street.

'You know I have to be at Elsternwick Park for the first football training session,' she says. 'I can't believe you're doing this to me, Rita. It's so unfair!'

Rita ignores her.

'Are you going to even answer me?' Maggie huffs, stomping her foot. 'I'm not going with you!'

'For goodness sake,' Rita snaps back. 'We're not going to Judith's, and we're not going to knit! Now hurry along!'

'We're not?' Maggie says, confused, chasing after her sister.

When Maggie and Rita reach the steps of the St Kilda Town Hall, Rita places the basket of yarn at her feet and waits in the shade between the towering colonnades.

'What are we doing here?' Maggie asks, just as four young ladies run up the steps towards them.

'This is my maddening little sister,' Rita says to them, giving a quick tug at Maggie's plaits. 'Maggie, these are my colleagues from the sewing factory. This is Eileen, Doris, Florence . . . and you already know Judith.'

It's only then that Maggie notices they are all in hockey tunics and flat oxford shoes.

'They're here to play football,' Rita adds. 'But not me. Not a chance! I'm off to see Terry.'

Maggie flings her arms around Rita. 'Thank you. Thank you. Thank you!' she cries.

But suddenly she has a terrible thought. She's left Patrick's footy behind on her bed. 'Oh, no! I didn't bring the footy!'

'Yes, you did.' Rita grins, reaching into the basket and taking out a football.

Maggie's face beams brighter than a lighthouse.

As they approach the entrance to Elsternwick Park, Maggie finds it hard to contain her excitement. She sprints ahead of Rita's friends and bolts out onto the oval.

She spots Ivy first. She's chatting to Marian and Annette. When she reaches them, Maggie is joined by Nancy and her five 1933 teammates. A few minutes later, Miss Kelly arrives with Lizzie, who's also brought along five of her workmates from the ammunition factory in Footscray and two more women who came to the store asking to join in. One has read the notice stuck up in Miss Kelly's store window and the other was at the dance and heard Gerald's announcement.

As the women are all getting acquainted, Nora appears. She's out of breath and runs up to Maggie.

'Thanks for coming,' Maggie says to her, hugging her.

'Well, with our Great Derby Secret Mission in place, how could I not?' Nora grins.

Maggie looks around, hoping that she'll see Elena. But there's no one else.

She does a quick head count. 'Twenty-four, including me,' she says, under her breath. 'But I can't count

Miss Kelly, so that's twenty-three all up.'

There are still not enough players to field two sides.

She puts her hands together in prayer. 'Thank you, Mary. You really are a true footy fan. And I really appreciate this so much. A-women.'

'So, Maggie,' says Ivy. 'We're here. Now what would you like us to do?'

'Do?' Maggie gulps, as everyone looks in her direction.

'May I, Maggie?' Nancy steps in. 'I think before we begin, we should all show our appreciation to Maggie, for showing courage, gumption and real passion to make this happen.'

They all clap enthusiastically, causing Maggie to blush.

'We don't have quite enough players for a full game, but we still have a week to find others,' adds Nancy. 'And if we don't manage that, then we'll get by with two teams of eleven players on each side and one sub, instead of eighteen players a team.'

Nancy shares her experience from playing in the 1933 charity game, and talks them through the training drills they did to prepare for that match.

When Miss Kelly suggests that Nancy should be the coach, everyone agrees.

'But even if we don't get full numbers, we'll need another coach,' she adds. 'Any takers?'

'I'll put my hand up – if you'll have me.'

Maggie can't believe it! She turns to see Grumpy Gaffney limping towards them.

'Yes! Yes!' she says excitedly.

Maggie introduces her neighbour to everyone and tells them about his war-time football experience.

'Well, Mr Gaffney, I was about to start with the basics, kicking and marking. So we can see what we have here in terms of skills,' says Nancy. 'What do you think?'

'Sounds about right to me,' Grumpy Gaffney says.

'But before you start,' Miss Kelly cuts in, taking out a Kodak box camera from her handbag. 'I want to capture this auspicious moment. Could I please have you all bunch up together for a picture?'

Once the photograph is taken, everyone breaks apart and runs into lines of two groups, facing each other.

'Take your kick, and go to the back of the line,' says Nancy.

Maggie begins at the front of her group. She punts the ball to Nancy, who heads up the opposing line, twenty metres away. Nancy marks the ball easily onto her chest. Maggie drops back to the end of her line, and watches Nancy drop kick the ball back to Marian.

Oh my, she thinks. She's brilliant! Ivy, Annette and Lizzie are strong players too. Marian is a little unsure at marking, but her kicks are solid. And some of the other women are a bit rusty, a couple of them are kicking the football for the first time, but they'll get the hang of it. And Nora . . .

Maggie grins.

'Nora! You're terrific!' she yells.

They run through drills, and as they start a practice match, Maggie has to pinch herself. This feels like a dream, a marvellous, glorious, feet-floating-off-the-ground dream.

But her dream is shattered by a sharp whistle. It sounds across the oval.

Two policemen are marching towards them.

'Stop!' they shout. 'Stop this at once!'

21

'What's the problem, officers?' asks Miss Kelly, who's been standing on the sidelines, next to Grumpy Gaffney.

The players gather around them.

'What's going on here?' asks one of the officers, the taller of the two.

'We're training for a footy match,' says Grumpy Gaffney. 'Can't you see that?'

'Football? Women playing football?' the other officer says.

'Yes, women,' Grumpy Gaffney says. 'It's a charity game for the troops.'

The officers exchange bewildered looks.

'It's not against the law for a girl to kick a football, is it?' says Ivy.

'Not technically, no,' says the taller policeman.

'But it is against the law to kick a ball in this park on Sundays. Didn't you see the sign?'

Maggie's heart sinks.

The officer points to the far end of the oval, where there's a big wooden sign lying flat on the ground.

'Aw, Bert! The sign's been knocked over,' the officer grumbles to his partner. 'Go get it, will ya?'

The shorter policeman jogs off and returns with the sign and shows it to everyone. It reads:

Elsternwick Park – Committee of Management.

The Playing of Games in This Park on Sundays is Not Allowed.

J. H. Taylor. Hon. Sec.

Maggie looks at Miss Kelly. They've been caught out.

Miss Kelly steps forward. 'I'm sorry, officers. If you are going to blame or fine anyone, it has to me,' she says. 'I arranged this gathering.'

Maggie shakes her head. 'I can't let you take the blame, Miss Kelly. I'm the one who has to be fined. This was my idea!'

'All right, all right. Ease up!' says the taller policeman. 'No one is getting fined this time. But this is a warning – to all of you. You girls go home now. Sundays are best spent in the kitchen.'

Lizzie and her friends from the factory look furious. Ivy looks like she's going to say something, but Nancy puts her hand on her arm and shakes her head.

The officers march off.

'Sorry, ladies,' Grumpy Gaffney says. 'What a pair of clowns. But at least we got in one training session before the actual game.'

'Please don't forget to ask around for more players,' Nancy exclaims.

'And tell everyone you know about the game,' says Marian. 'We want to raise as much money as we can. I'll tell everyone on my milk run.'

'I'll spread the word on my ice route,' adds Ivy.

'And I'll tell everyone who comes to the theatre this week,' says Annette.

'It goes without saying that everyone who comes into the store will hear about it too,' exclaims Miss Kelly.

Maggie and her teammates say goodbye and separate. Maggie walks home in silence with Grumpy Gaffney and Nora by her side, bouncing the ball every couple of steps.

'Maggie, please!' says Grumpy Gaffney. 'I know you're feeling flat about not being able to play for long today, but we did get some training in and you can look forward to next week.'

'It's going to be great, Maggie,' says Nora. 'I thought everyone was really good!'

As they turn into the street, Maggie spots an Army jeep parked outside her house.

'Huh?' she says. 'What's that doing there?'

Gerald and his mother and Nan are standing out front on the footpath.

Maggie runs ahead. As she pushes through the front gate, an Army officer steps away from the doorway and brushes past her. In the doorway, her mother is sobbing into her father's chest.

'What's going on?' Maggie asks. 'Who was that?'

'It's about Pat,' says her dad. 'I'm afraid it's bad news, Carrots.'

'He's missing!' Maggie's mother blurts in between sobs. 'Missing in action.'

'But they'll find him, right?' Maggie asks, breathless. 'If he's missing, they can find him.'

'It's been quite a while,' Maggie's father says. 'That's why we haven't had letters.'

Maggie has never seen her father close to tears before.

Maggie looks back to see Nora, Gerald, his mother and Nan, and Grumpy Gaffney gathered at the gate.

'He was a part of some covert mission,' Maggie's

father says. 'And details are only filtering through.'

'But they *are* going to find him, right?' Maggie asks, feeling the panic rise into her throat. 'Right?' Maggie's hands are trembling, and she feels weak at the knees.

'Why aren't you answering me, Dad?' she cries. 'They *will* find him, won't they?'

But Maggie knows the answer.

Missing in action most likely means he's dead.

We've been merrily going on with life, imagining that he's out there flying, she thinks, not at all aware of what's happened. I've written him letters that he'll never get!

'He's not dead!' Maggie yells. 'He's not! He can't be!'

Clutching her football, Maggie turns, pushes her way through everyone at the front gate, and bolts down the street.

'Maggie!' Gerald cries, chasing after her.

Maggie runs. And she doesn't stop running.

Everything is a blur. Except for Patrick. She sees him. She sees his smile. She hears his voice. His laugh.

She's not going anywhere – she's just running, tears racing down her cheeks.

She runs through the streets and as far as the large

open-mouthed clown face of Luna Park. She runs past the arched roof and twin-domed towers of the Palais picture theatre.

When she reaches the beach, there's nowhere left to run. She slows to a walk and then drops to the sand. She sits by the water, exhausted, doubled over sobbing.

'Maggie?' Gerald puffs, finally catching up to her, pushing his curls out of his eyes.

Maggie looks up, sniffling.

Gerald crouches down and puts his arm around her. Which just makes Maggie cry even more.

22

For the next couple of days, Maggie steers clear of everyone. She doesn't want to talk to anyone at school, even though it seems like everyone knows and wants to talk to her about Patrick.

The newspapers are filled with the news that the Dutch East Indies has been occupied and Java has fallen. Attacks on New Guinea mean the fighting is getting closer and closer. Maggie's dad has stopped talking about the war at dinner and the wireless stays off at night now.

'I heard about your brother, Maggie,' says Frances, stepping up to her at lunchtime on Wednesday. 'I assume you'll want a few days to grieve and won't want to participate in the charity events this Saturday.'

'Wouldn't you just love that?' Maggie says. 'I'm not sure who made you queen of our school, but you can assume as much as you like. You don't know what I'm feeling, and I'll still be participating. Now excuse me, I'm off to see someone who does know me!'

But the truth is, Maggie doesn't want to do anything at all.

Running away from Frances as quickly as she can, Maggie feels as if she can't breathe.

She makes her way towards Sister Gertrude's office. When the coast is clear, she ducks inside and looks up at the portrait of Mary.

'Dear Mary, Mother of God. I need your help again,' Maggie says. 'There must be some mistake, because I know you wouldn't've let this happen. You helped me find players and you helped Gerald to get up on stage, so Patrick *can't* be dead. He's missing, and that means he can be found, so please find him for me, for my family.'

'What do you think you're doing?'

Maggie whips around to see Sister Gertrude looming over her.

'I . . . I . . .' she stammers. 'I'm praying.'

'Is this about your brother?' Sister Gertrude asks, making her way around to her desk.

Maggie nods.

'Sister Clare told me the news,' she says, rummaging through her desk drawer. 'War is unforgiving.

People lose their lives.'

Maggie feels her blood start to boil. Her heart is racing. How can Sister Gertrude say that? How can she brush it off as if it's nothing?

Sister Gertrude pulls out her cane.

'Are you going to punish me for standing in your office?'

'No,' Sister Gertrude snaps. 'But I should. The cane's not for you. It's for him!'

Maggie turns to see Mickey standing in the doorway. She almost feels sorry for him.

But why should I? she thinks. The horrible things he's said to me, Gerald and Elena are unforgivable.

'Mickey Mulligan, you continue to be one big disappointment, don't you?' Sister Gertrude says.

Maggie catches Mickey's eye, but it's impossible to tell if he's scared or upset or angry. Impossible to tell if he's feeling anything at all.

Grown-ups keep saying things like that to him, she thinks. They put him down, so he puts us down.

'Why are you still here, Maggie Flanagan?' Sister Gertrude growls, placing her cane on her desk. 'Leave my office now!'

Suddenly a wave of fury and sadness washes over Maggie. Her entire body shakes as she imagines Patrick being shot out of the sky and spiralling down . . . and down . . . and down.

'It's not fair!' she screams, startling Sister Gertrude and Mickey. 'It's not fair! It's not fair! It's not fair!'

Maggie snatches the cane off the desk and snaps it across her knee. Mickey looks on, flabbergasted.

Sister Gertrude looks as if she's about to go up in flames.

Maggie charges out of the office, into the courtyard and through the school's front gate and runs all the way home.

23

'All right, it's Saturday morning and you can't stay in bed forever,' Rita exclaims, standing over Maggie.

Maggie can't see Rita as she has the covers pulled over her head. She's barely left her room.

'So you were suspended from school for a couple of days, but that doesn't mean you can't talk or eat or see your family. And I can't keep saying to Gerald, "Come back again later!" This isn't you, Maggie. You have to somehow keep going. We all do, no matter how painful this is.'

Maggie squirms but still doesn't say a word.

'Judith said to say that you're the whole reason the football match is even happening today and they need you to be there. Come on, Maggie. You've been dreaming of this day forever. Pat would want you to play.'

'Football isn't football, if there's no Patrick,' Maggie

mumbles from under the sheets.

'Of course, it is.' Rita sighs. 'Football will help us keep Pat's memory alive.'

Maggie's head slowly emerges from under the covers. Her eyes are puffy and red. She peers up at her sister.

Rita looks as though she's been crying too. She leans down to hug Maggie.

'I know isn't easy,' Rita says softly, just as their mother bursts into the room waving a newspaper in her hand.

'What's this?' she asks, her voice cracking.

'A newspaper?' Maggie says.

'I know it's a newspaper,' her mother snaps. 'It's an article in the newspaper! About you!'

'About me?'

Maggie's mother reads the article out loud:

Look out, boys. Here come the footy girls!

Twelve-year-old Maggie Flanagan of St Kilda isn't your everyday girl – happy to play with dolls or dress-ups. Instead, she is most content when she is kicking a football. She adores footy as much as any boy and wishes she could play in a real team. Today she just might get her chance. She has been the driving force behind the formation of an all-female football match to raise money for the troops. But to do that, they need you!

Official ball-up is at 2pm today at Elsternwick Park. This is most certainly a worthy cause, and if you are curious to see how girls take on a boys' game, then this is definitely the event for you.

Maggie can't believe it.

Rita snatches the paper out of her mother's hands. 'There's even a photo of you, Maggie!' she squeals excitedly. 'How did they get a photo of you?'

Maggie thinks of Miss Kelly and her Kodak box camera from last Sunday's training in Elsternwick Park.

'Maggie, how could you?' Their mother is clearly upset. 'Doing all of this behind our backs? What were you thinking? Football! And then there's your outrageous behaviour at school this week, breaking canes and causing havoc. It's hard enough for me with the news of Patrick. This is too much for me to handle. Do you understand me? I forbid you to play!'

'Mum, you've got to let her,' Rita pleads.

'No, that's my final word on the subject,' she says, turning and marching out of the room, brushing past Maggie's father in the doorway.

'Girls, best you leave it alone,' he says, shaking his head. 'None of this is easy for her.' He sighs. 'It's not easy for any of us. Let me talk to her about the football match, all right? But for now, Carrots, you need to go.'

'Go where?'

'Your school's fundraising event. You committed to it so I expect you to go. Get dressed. Gerald's waiting outside with his billycart.'

—

When Maggie and Gerald arrive at the top of the Barkly Street hill, there's a large crowd milling around the cake and sewing stalls at the bottom of the steep road. They run down to join everyone.

The girls in Maggie's class are already split up into groups and are manning the stalls. Frances looks totally in her element, bossing others to help Sister Agnes carry around trays of scones, chocolate ripple cake and honey-and-ginger biscuits.

The boys are wheeling their billycarts around like thoroughbreds in the mounting yard at the Melbourne Cup. They're lapping up the attention from the adults who are admiring their racing jalopies. There's even an announcer, Frances's grandfather, who is shouting into a megaphone.

'Ladies and Gentlemen, don't forget that all the proceeds from today go to our diggers, so buy your cakes, your sweets, and have your socks and shirts sewn . . . and don't forget to donate your loose change to the young people wandering around with collection tins. This is sure to be the greatest billycart derby this side of the Yarra. The racing heats start in just half an hour.'

All of the boys participating in the derby are wearing motorcycle helmets and goggles. Mickey and Jimmy are excitedly hip-and-shouldering each other as if they can't wait a minute longer.

Gerald and Maggie run through the plan for the Great Derby Secret Mission.

'Do you really think it will work?' asks Gerald.

Maggie scans the crowd and spots Nora shadowing Frances, as she usually does.

Nora notices Maggie looking at her and waves.

'Fingers crossed,' says Maggie as Gerald wheels his billycart away.

Nora breaks away from Frances, and joins Gerald in the group of billycart riders.

Father Finney is handing out numbered bibs to each of them.

'Oh, Maggie, I'm so glad you decided to show up this morning,' says Sister Clare, tapping her on the shoulder. 'You and your family have been in my prayers all week.'

'Thank you, Sister,' Maggie replies.

'And I know you're not so keen on sewing,' she adds,

handing her a tin bucket. 'So, how about you be one of the collection handlers instead? It's also a good way to keep out of Sister Gertrude's path, if you know what I mean.'

As Maggie wanders through the ever-growing crowd, collecting donations, Frances's grandfather makes another announcement. He is now standing on a stepladder, holding a pair of binoculars in one hand, and his trusty megaphone in the other.

'Ladies and Gentlemen, Boys and Girls, the time has arrived. The billycart derby is about to begin.'

Everyone cheers. Maggie looks up towards the top of the steep street, where the Grade Five and Six boys have gathered with their billycarts.

'There will be five heats, with the winner from each heat qualifying for the final derby race. And it looks as if heat one is about to begin. And they're off and racing!'

24

Maggie pushes through to the front of the crowd.

'And Danny O'Leary races out in front . . . but here comes Paul McMahon, leaving the others in his dust. Side by side, it looks as if McMahon and O'Leary will take it to the line . . . and it's . . . McMahon by a wheel! Paul McMahon, from Grade Five, is our first heat winner!'

Frances's grandfather calls the second heat, and it's won by a Grade Six boy called Val Rogers.

In the third heat, Mickey tramples over his opponents and it looks as if he's the fastest winner so far.

In the fourth heat, Jimmy is the victor by a long way.

When it comes to the final heat, Maggie crosses her fingers.

'And they're off . . .' cries Frances's grandfather.

'And this is the closest contest of them all, folks! Sean Mullins inches ahead of Joe O'Donnell and Danny Flaherty, and just behind them is Gerald Fitzgerald. This is neck and neck . . .'

'Go! Go! Go!' Maggie yells.

'They swerve and bump . . . and, oh, this is going to come down to the wire. Flaherty, O'Donnell are looking very good, but here comes Fitzgerald! Fitzgerald, O'Donnell and Flaherty . . . they come in together . . . but . . . Gerald Fitzgerald wins by half a bee's bottom!'

'Yes! Yes!' Maggie screams excitedly.

Gerald has made it into the final.

In no time at all, the finalists make their way back to the top of the hill. The excitement is swelling, and the crowd continues to grow. Maggie does another quick collection run. Her tin bucket is over three quarters full. She manages to position herself in a prime viewing spot – this time right by the finishing line.

'This is the moment we've been waiting for, Ladies and Gentlemen, Boys and Girls. Be sure to make plenty of noise and barrack for these boys as they line up for the race of their young lives. And thank you again to everyone who has donated for this wonderful fundraising cause. We hope you have enjoyed the cake and sewing stalls, and these hair-raising races. And it's time to see who the ultimate winner will be.'

As Maggie takes a deep breath, someone pushes through the crowd and bumps her arm. He's wearing a fedora hat tilted over his eyes. It's Gerald!

'You're supposed to be hiding.' Maggie laughs.

'I couldn't resist seeing the final,' he says, pulling his father's hat further down over his face. 'No one suspects a thing. The helmet and goggles are the perfect disguise. No one has even taken a second look at Nora. And it proves that they mostly just ignore me! Your Great Derby Secret Mission might just work, Maggie. It's fantastic she won the heat. Let's hope she can win the final.'

'And they're off again . . . the fastest and the best . . . Paul McMahon is quick to take the lead, followed by Jimmy Noonan, Mickey Mulligan, Val Rogers, and the slow-to-start Gerald Fitzgerald. And boy, oh boy, they are travelling at breakneck speed, folks. Mulligan whizzes out in front, alongside Noonan, while Rogers and McMahon drop back. But look out! Here comes Gerald Fitzgerald, making his move and inching forward, right on the tail of Mulligan and Noonan.'

'GO! GO!' Maggie and Gerald shout at the top of their lungs.

'Oh no! McMahon has lost control of his steering and has crashed into the crowd. We do hope everyone is all right. This is going to be oh so close. Jimmy Noonan forges ahead, and Fitzgerald swiftly moves into second position, with Mulligan just behind them. It's Noonan, Fitzgerald . . . Fitzgerald, Noonan . . . Noonan, Fitzgerald . . . and, oh my goodness, it's . . . FITZGERALD! Gerald Fitzgerald is our champion!'

The crowd cheers and swarms around the racers as they roll to a stop past the finishing line.

Nora jumps up and down with excitement.

'Maggie!' she yells. 'Gerald! I did it! I actually did it!' She pulls off her helmet and goggles, and the crowd gasps.

Frances squeals in horror.

Maggie and Gerald push through the crowd and hug Nora.

'What is the meaning of this?' Sister Gertrude bellows, bursting through the spectators. 'You! Of course it's you, Maggie Flanagan. Of course you're behind this malarkey! Just as you have been behind *this*!'

Sister Gertrude holds up the newspaper article.

'Girls playing football? What an embarrassment to us all,' she exclaims. 'No, I'm not having any of it.

Nora, you are disqualified, and, Maggie, I ban you and any other female pupils from playing a man's game.'

'Oh, Gertie, honestly!' Sister Agnes appears alongside Sister Gertrude. 'I have known you since you were a girl, and it's time to drop this nonsense. Look around you. How many young men do you see here? They're all off at war. Everyone expects the girls to step up and do the work these days. Can't they have some of the fun too? Tomorrow I turn eighty, and I've seen a lot of change. And a lot of billycart driving. But, Nora, that was the most extraordinary billycart driving I've ever seen.'

'I agree,' Father Finney exclaims. 'Nora is our winner today. And I think we should embrace Maggie's initiative. After all, it's for a good cause.'

'Hear, hear!' calls Sister Clare.

Maggie can't believe what she's hearing. Sister Gertrude is completely lost for words, and for the first time appears not to know what to do.

Maggie's father weaves his way through the crowd.

'We're behind you all the way, Carrots,' he calls. 'Go for it.'

Maggie looks out into the crowd and sees George giving her the thumbs-up. She catches her breath.

Gerald laughs and whacks her on the arm.

'Snap out of it, Miss Smitten! Your face is as bright red as Rita's lipstick,' he says. 'You've got a football match to play.'

25

Maggie swallows her nerves as she and her dad approach Elsternwick Park.

'Strewth! Look at the turn-out!' her father remarks.

Maggie can't believe it. Several thousand people have shown up, all lining the boundary of the park oval.

'It's like a VFA crowd,' she says, her stomach swirling with butterflies.

She looks up at her dad. 'Will Mum forgive me?' she asks. 'She said I couldn't go.'

'She might not be here, Carrots, and she might not approve, but she told me and Rita to come to watch you so I think it's all right.'

Maggie and her father snake their way through the spectators and step onto the oval.

'There she is!' cries Nancy, bounding over to greet her. 'Maggie, I'm so sorry to hear about your brother. We're so pleased you're here. Look at all this support. Incredible, right? And over there! Look! That article in the *Argus* really did the trick.'

Maggie feels as if she is floating. She tries to take in as much as she can, as quick as she can, to ground herself.

'Your guernsey!' she says, pointing at Nancy's maroon jumper. 'Where did you get that?'

All the players are wearing uniforms. One group has steel-blue guernseys with a white map of Australia on the front. The other team has maroon jumpers with a white kangaroo emblem.

Then Maggie recognises the gear – they're the same guernseys she saw in Grumpy Gaffney's photograph, the ones that he and his Army buddies wore in the London exhibition game.

'And, look!' says Lizzie. 'Almost all of us are wearing shorts. Most of the girls are wearing them for the very first time.'

She hands Maggie a pair of navy shorts. 'Your sister and the girls at her work made them for us. She made you one too, of course. You can pull them on under your skirt.'

'Some of the old blokes in the audience think it's

outrageous,' says Miss Kelly. 'I heard one of them say, "A sea of knees! So unladylike. What's this world coming to?"'

Maggie laughs.

'Your brother would be proud of you, Maggie,' Grumpy Gaffney says, holding up one of the maroon guernseys. 'And I am too.'

'Mr Gaffney, are these jumpers . . .'

'Yes, the very same,' he says, handing Maggie the guernsey. 'I can't think of a better way to honour all the boys who went to war.'

Maggie thanks Grumpy Gaffney and squeezes her dad's hand.

'You're going to be on my side, Maggie,' Nancy says. 'We're calling ourselves the Miss-fits. Get it? And Mr Gaffney's team are the Belles. We thought we'd put you in the goal square, hoping you'll kick a bag of goals. How does that sound?'

Maggie nods excitedly.

'And the good news is we have one new player – she saw the sign in the window – and we've roped in a couple of players you might already know,' says Grumpy Gaffney, gesturing back towards the two teams.

Emerging from out of the huddle is Elena.

'If the Melbourne Demons could have Ronald

Barassi and St Kilda can have a Cyril Gambetta, then I think this match should have a Spinelli,' she says. 'I know you were trying to help. So I decided to help too.'

Maggie throws herself at Elena and hugs her tightly.

But then she sees something that makes her jaw drop. It's Sister Clare. She still has her veil and wimple on her head, but she's wearing a maroon jumper over her usual black tunic.

'It's all right, Maggie,' she says, smiling. 'Don't look so shocked. I'm happy to have Father Finney's blessing to be able to play today, and I love kicking a footy as much as the next nun.'

'It was you!' Maggie cries. 'You were the mystery kicker at the convent the day I was sweeping the verandah. The kick from behind the rose bushes.'

Sister Clare grins. 'That was me. This is going to be so much fun.'

Gerald, Frances and George saunter up. Maggie is surprised to see them all together, especially Frances – who seems to have dragged her grandfather along, complete with megaphone.

'Just so you know, I'm here for Nora,' she says. 'And Grandpa Desmond said I should come to show my support for the troops. Not for you. Got it?'

'Loud and clear,' Maggie says, shaking her head.

'Also,' Frances adds, 'Grandpa Desmond loved calling the billycart derby so much that he's volunteering to call this game, too.'

Frances waves to Nora, who is surrounded by her Belles teammates.

'Frances and I are going to collect donations,' Gerald cuts in, swinging two collection buckets. 'She agreed to help me.'

'I didn't,' Frances snaps. 'But Sister Clare said if I helped, she'd let me be classroom monitor for an entire week. So there!'

'And I'm going to umpire the game,' says George. 'I'm happy to help you out, Maggie.'

Maggie nods, trying not to appear too flustered as his blue eyes twinkle and he smiles at her. She wonders if she'll be able to concentrate during the match with him running around.

She catches Gerald making a kissy face at her and laughing.

'Maggie!' Miss Kelly calls out to her. 'Photograph time!'

Maggie runs to join her teammates. She kneels in the front row, holding the football – as Miss Kelly captures the two teams poised and raring to go.

'Ladies and Gentlemen, Boys and Girls, welcome!'

shouts Grandpa Desmond into his megaphone. 'Welcome to this historic charity event. Football like you've never seen it played before. Prepare to be enthralled as we witness the Mighty Miss-fits take on the Fighting Belles.'

As Nancy and Grumpy Gaffney call in their respective teams and give their pre-match address, Maggie almost can't believe it.

It's happening. It's really happening!

If only Patrick were here to see it.

26

The players run on to the oval. Maggie sprints to the goal square to take up her position as full forward. She's joined by her opponent, Annette.

'Isn't this just brilliant, Maggie?' Annette says. 'It's better than all the VFL grand finals put together.'

George blows his whistle. The crowd erupts into one giant hurrah.

Maggie shuffles back and forth, keeping distance between her and Annette, ready to bolt and lead for the ball. But the play already seems to be stalled in the middle of the ground.

Both sides bump and jostle, never really holding the ball much longer than a few seconds.

For the first few minutes of the game, nerves and jitters overwhelm the players on both sides. Some of the crowd begin to laugh and taunt.

Grandpa Desmond calls the scrappy play.

'This might not look like the football we're famil-iar with, folks. It does appear, for now, that players are struggling to find a clear break, content to kick the ball mostly along the ground. At this early stage they look like children who have been let loose in the back-yard on an Easter egg hunt.'

Maggie turns to a group of grey-haired old men standing directly behind the goals. They're yelling and laughing at her and Annette. She glares at them.

'Just ignore them, Maggie,' says Annette, her stare fixed on the play in the middle of the ground. 'Let them laugh. They're nervous that we might play bet-ter than they ever did. Focus on the game.'

Maggie nods. It's good advice.

'And the Belles finally get it out of the centre and kick it long into the forward line, and it really is a fine kick by my milkman, sorry, milk-woman, Mrs Stewart.' Grandpa Desmond's animated voice echoes across the park. 'And the mark is taken by the full forward for the Belles. Sorry, folks, I don't know all the players' names . . .'

Maggie looks over to Frances's grandfather, who is standing on his stepladder with his megaphone. Miss Kelly tugs at his arm. She appears to be telling him something.

'Ladies and Gentlemen, the full forward for the Belles is Miss Lizzie Nolan . . . and Miss Nolan puts it through for the first score of the match.'

For the rest of the quarter, the game continues to be a hodgepodge of stop-and-start kicks and tackles. Maggie is frustrated that the ball has not once come her way, and that her team hasn't kicked a single point.

No one's skills are on display. Playing in front of a hostile crowd is making it hard to play their best game.

'And that ends the first quarter . . . with the Belles leading the Miss-fits by two goals, two goals to nothing.'

At the break, the teams huddle close together.

'I know you're all nervous, but I want some clean and direct passage of play.' Nancy addresses the Miss-fits. 'Look around you before you charge in with blinkers on. Elena, you have great spring in your legs. Are you sure you're not part kangaroo? I'm swapping you with Ivy. You're playing in the ruck.'

Maggie can hear Grumpy Gaffney revving up the Belles too.

'Spread out. Ceate some run for yourself and your teammates . . . Don't second-guess. Go in with guts and confidence. And get the ball out of the middle as quick as you can! Sister Clare, I think in this case you'll have to do unto others as they most certainly will do unto you. And in this case that means don't hold back. If they bump you, you bump them right back. Hard! Got it?'

Sister Clare nods nervously and makes the sign of the cross.

Shuffling through the huddled players, Sister Agnes carries a tray of ginger biscuits left over from the fundraiser stalls. Most of Maggie's teammates politely decline, but Maggie jams three into her mouth.

'All that running out there has made you ravenous, dear,' Sister Agnes says. 'Jesus, Mary and Joseph, I thought I'd never see something so magnificent in my lifetime. If I were a couple of years younger, I'd be out there with you. Keep up the good work, girls!'

The second quarter is better all round. Sister Clare puts her skills on display and turns out to be very fast with the ball, even with her black veil streaming behind her like a kind of cape.

Then Rita's best friend Judith contests the footy in a ball-up, taps it on to Florence, who swiftly handballs to Maggie. It's her first touch of the ball all game!

'Young Maggie Flanagan twists and turns and easily outruns her opponent,' Grandpa Desmond bellows. 'She takes a nervous snap for goal, but, oh . . . off the side of the boot it goes. A ghastly punt. Out on the full!

And there goes the whistle! Halftime, folks.'

Maggie feels like the world has just collapsed on her.

Elena runs up beside her. 'Don't worry, Maggie. It's sure to put some fire under you in the second half. You'll get past it!'

—

'Ladies and Gentlemen, your generosity is unsurpassed,' Grandpa Desmond announces, as the teams run back out onto the oval to begin the third quarter. 'The collection count so far is an astounding one hundred and ten pounds. The football skills on display might be below par, but the giving is most certainly not.'

'Below par?' Maggie mutters. 'The nerve!'

'Come on, everyone,' she shouts as she jogs back into the goal square. 'Let's show them what we're made of!'

'Sugar and spice,' jokes one of the old men from behind the goals. The surrounding spectators burst out laughing – including Mickey and Jimmy, who have shown up to taunt them.

'Where are ya high heels, Flanagan?' Mickey shouts, making the men crack up again.

But the second half is a different game. Maggie can

see that the taunts from the sidelines are making the girls so angry that they forget their nerves.

Elena's powerful jumping ability helps her dominate in the ball-up. She gets her fist to the footy and thumps it out of the centre to a roving Sister Clare, who fires a steady kick to the right forward pocket, where it's marked by Judith. Judith decides to play on, and drop kicks the ball directly to Maggie, who leads for it and marks it firmly.

Maggie exhales. Her heart is racing, but she feels strong and in control. It's the most in control she's felt in a long time. She goes back to take her kick.

She knows it's good the second her foot touches the ball. It's measured, it's direct and it's beautiful.

The ball soars right through the middle of the big sticks.

The crowd cheers.

'And the Mighty Miss-fits are in the game!' cries Grandpa Desmond. 'A result of the best passage of play we've seen so far in this match.'

The crowd's jokes and jeers begin to fade, as they realise they're witnessing a classic competition between two spirited and skilful sides.

The third quarter is a goal-for-goal showdown. Maggie can't tell if the old men by the goals have been silenced, because the crowd is going so wild that it would be impossible to hear them.

With the positivity from the crowd, everyone's skills and passion lift. By the end of the quarter, breathtaking combinations of kicks, marks and tackles are on display. Maggie finds her stride and boots three more goals, one after the other.

From the sidelines, she can hear Gerald shout, 'Go, Maggie!' He's cheering alongside Rita and Maggie's father, who is smiling proudly.

Gerald starts singing *Oh, My Darling Clementine* at the top of his lungs, and Maggie smiles when she realises that he's changed the words to 'Oh, My Maggie, Friend of Mine'. He grabs Rita and waltzes her around and around.

———

When the Belles and Miss-fits return to the field to play the final quarter, the spectators are buzzing, hoping for an exciting finish to a history-making match.

'Yes, Ladies and Gentlemen, I'm as surprised as you are. This is turning out to be a marvellous sporting spectacle and a brilliant display of our magnificent game,' Grandpa Desmond says, his voice sounding raspy after a long day of shouting.

'That's more like it,' Maggie says under her breath.

'The score is the fighting Belles 8.4(52) to the mighty Miss-fits 7.7(49), but will we see more goals before it rains? I don't like the look of those dark clouds heading this way. I hope you've all packed your brollies and hats.'

The final quarter is a hard slog for both sides.

Everyone, including Maggie, is beginning to tire. But despite the fatigue, neither team is willing to concede. Nora kicks two more goals for the Belles. And Ivy kicks two more for the Miss-fits.

Ivy gives Maggie a thumbs-up. Maggie grins and waves back at her.

'With barely any time remaining, here comes the rain, folks!' cries Grandpa Desmond.

The heavens open, and heavy rain drenches everyone. Within minutes, the firm, grass-covered oval is transformed into one giant muddy puddle. But the play continues.

Maggie can't see more than a foot in front of her. Both sides are slipping and sliding. Everyone is finding it difficult to get a grip on the ball. They resort to kicking the waterlogged footy off the ground, desperately trying to inch it in the direction of their goals. But the downpour doesn't dampen the enthusiasm of the crowd. In fact, it only spurs them on to cheer even harder.

When the storm begins to ease up, the Miss-fits gain possession of the ball. Elena baulks and weaves past three Belles, and boots the footy to Sister Clare.

Sister Clare marks it, sidesteps her opponent, and lets loose with an almighty kick. It's a punt to rival the one that Maggie witnessed at the convent.

Maggie and Annette both run for the ball, ploughing their way through the mud. Annette loses her footing and slips, while Maggie desperately dives forward, her arms fully extended.

It feels like time has slowed down.

She cups the football in her arms, pulls it in firmly to her chest . . . and hits the muddy turf with a thud.

George blows sharply on his whistle to signal the end of the match.

The crowd cheers, wildly applauding the spectacular grab.

Maggie looks desperately at George. Will she be allowed to take her kick for goal?

He signals that she will.

'Oh my! Oh my!' cries Grandpa Desmond. 'The Miss-fits are three points behind, and if Maggie Flanagan makes this kick, they will snatch victory from the Belles. Talk about a dramatic ending, Ladies and Gentlemen. Flanagan's gutsy mark is one that any man would be proud of.'

Maggie gets to her feet, covered in sludge from head to toe. She wipes the grass and muck off her face, takes a deep breath and prepares to take her kick.

She looks between the posts and picks an imaginary spot in the sky. She points the footy down at a ninety-degree angle. Her cold fingers spread wide, around the ball.

Stepping forward, she kicks it with all her might. The heavy wet ball wobbles high above the opposition player on the mark.

And right through the middle of the sticks!

'And she does it! You ripper!' Grandpa Desmond hollers. 'The Miss-fits are the victors. But *all* the ladies are the winners today!'

Maggie's teammates rush forward and encircle her, hugging each other and jumping for joy. Even the players from the Belles dash over to join in the celebration. Ivy and Nancy hoist Maggie onto their shoulders.

'Three cheers for Maggie!' they shout.

'Hip-hip hooray! Hip-hip hooray! Hip-hip hooray!' everyone cries.

Maggie thrusts her arms up in the air, feeling every bit like one of her St Kilda football heroes. She has never felt so exhilarated in her entire life.

From Ivy and Nancy's shoulders she can see across the crowd. Everyone is wet and a bit muddy, but no one cares. They're all caught up in the frenzied jubilation.

But at the back of the crowd, Maggie sees something extraordinary. Something she never thought she'd see again.

She rubs her eyes to check if she's seeing things.

Her mother is standing on the boundary line, holding baby Colleen on her hip. And next to her is a young man in an Air Force uniform, waving frantically.

Maggie gasps, almost losing her balance and falling off her teammates' shoulders. Her heart beats quicker.

It's Patrick.

'Put me down! Put me down!' she screams.

Maggie charges for her big brother, tears streaming across her muddy face. She slams into his embrace and holds on as if she'll never let him go again.

27

'We went down just south of Sicily and were unable to make contact for a couple of weeks. The logistics to get us back home were, um . . . Let's just say, I was lucky to get out of there alive,' Patrick explains later that night. 'I'm sorry you had to go through what you did, Mum.'

Maggie's mother reaches across the kitchen table and squeezes Patrick's hand.

Rita leans over to kiss him on the cheek. 'Lucky she wouldn't give me your room, Pat. Even though I begged. Goodnight, brother. And don't you ever scare us like that again.'

Maggie has not let Patrick out of her sight since the game. With the match football on her lap, she sits gazing at him, hanging on every word he says.

She tries not to think about how much weight he's

lost. His arms are skinnier, and his face is gaunt. The prickly rusty-coloured stubble on his chin and neck make him look a lot older than he is.

He looks more like dad, she thinks.

'And the war in the Pacific?' Maggie's father asks, sounding concerned. 'Is it as bad as they say?'

'Yeah, Dad. It's really troubling.' Patrick nods. 'We need to hold New Guinea. You'll see more Australians sent over there. But the Americans are fighting hard in the air over the Pacific. We can expect more Yanks based here in Melbourne. The MCG has been requisitioned for military personnel. I'm afraid there'll be no footy season this year, Carrots,' he says.

'I think we've had enough footy drama and tears today to last us a lifetime,' Maggie's mother says, standing up from the table. 'It's time for me to call it a night too, Pat. Come on, Joe. Don't make him talk about the war any more.'

When it's just Patrick and Maggie in the kitchen, Maggie finally has the courage to ask what she's wanted to know from the second she saw Patrick at the football match.

'Do you really have to leave again?' Maggie asks, dreading the answer.

'Yes, I do,' he says. 'I head out next week.'

Maggie's stomach churns.

'But at least I'm around long enough for a kick-to-kick,' he adds, snatching the footy off her.

'Tomorrow?'

'You bet! And, Carrots . . . I'm so happy that I got to see the last few minutes of the game. You were marvellous.'

Maggie smiles. Hearing Patrick call her Carrots again, in person, makes her heart swell with happiness.

'All right, I think it's time for me to hit the sack,' he says.

'Can I ask you one more thing?' Maggie says.

She tells Patrick about the Japanese spy plane, about how no one else saw it and no one believed her.

'I was so afraid, Pat. Everyone tells me I imagined it, but I really don't think I did. Could it be true? Have you heard anything about it?'

'A Japanese aircraft?' Patrick repeats. 'Flying over Melbourne?'

There's a long pause before Patrick says anything else, but the look on his face doesn't make Maggie feel any better.

'I wasn't seeing things, was I?' she whispers.

'Look, I won't lie to you. I have heard talk from some of the boys at the Laverton airbase. I assumed it was just talk. But maybe it wasn't. So make sure you cover those windows at night, take the air raid drills seriously, and let's hope you were seeing things, all right?'

Maggie nods.

Patrick gets up from his chair, walks over to the doorway leading from the kitchen to the hallway, but then stops.

He turns, and handballs the football back to Maggie. 'I do believe Australia can come through,' he says. 'I really believe we can win this.'

Maggie grasps the footy firmly in her hands, and smiles.

'Me too,' she says.

28

In 1942, in the Melbourne suburb of St Kilda, a girl lies in the dark and prays.

She prays for her family.

She prays for her friends.

She prays for the war to be over.

And she prays for a world where girls can play football.

'A-women,' she whispers.

From the author

I've often said characters and their stories come and find you. Whenever I go in search of stories or push for a story to appear, it never does. Writing books for me has always meant stepping back, letting go and having faith that the ideas and characters will come when the time is right.

Back in 2019, I was visiting friends in the UK and while on a train to Scotland I came across a discarded newspaper on my seat and started reading it. There was an article in the sports section about women's football – soccer – during the First World War (which used to be called the Great War).

Matches played by women were hugely popular all over the UK at the time. It was fascinating to read how thousands turned out to watch these matches while the men were fighting overseas. One women's game at Everton had a crowd of 50 000 people!

But once the war was over, the Football Association was worried that the women's game would take money and attention away from the men's game, and women were banned from playing.

I began to wonder whether women in Australia had had a similar experience, but with Aussie Rules football . . .

Then 2020 hit, and we know where the entire world was that year – in lockdown! Back in Melbourne, Australia, I was on one of my daily walks at my local park when I bumped into an old friend. My friend told me how his daughter was a huge fan of Aussie Rules and the Specky Magee series and identified with the character of Tiger Girl. She hoped to one day play in the AFLW. My mind went back to the newspaper article about the history of women's soccer.

I rushed home and looked up 'Women in Australian Rules Football'. I was excited to learn that there were accounts of women playing Aussie Rules as far back as 1880. Before I knew it, I was researching all-female games that were played in 1918, in the 1920s, 30s and 40s.

Maggie's voice came to me loud and clear when I read about an all-women's game played as a wartime fundraiser in Perth in 1915. This is the game that Miss Kelly talks about.

You probably know how much I love my footy, but if I hadn't heard about this amazing piece of history, then I was sure lots of other people hadn't either.

While writing this book I learned so much about my city and about the culture of the 1940s. Most people didn't think that women could or should play contact sports, and they often thought that there were lots of jobs and activities that were only for men. The war changed all that. At least for a while.

After the war, the same things happened here to women who had taken jobs as had happened to the women footballers in the UK. They were expected to hand their jobs back to any man who wanted one.

I gained a deeper understanding of the challenges women faced during this era, and of how fear and ignorance could bring out the worst in people.

And it wasn't just difficult to be a girl who wanted something a bit different with your life. It was hard to be a boy who didn't fit the mould as well, like Gerald. It was also tough to be someone who didn't have a cultural background from the UK, like Elena. Yes, they really did lock up Italian Australians in camps, and they didn't have to prove that you had done anything wrong. Australia locked up

German and Japanese Australians too and many others.

But I also wanted to communicate the idea that it's often during a crisis that we come together with a sense of community spirit and show the very best of ourselves.

I wanted to place my story at a time when Australians felt directly threatened at home. That was definitely the case during the Second World War and most especially in 1942, the year British Singapore fell to the Japanese and northern Australia was attacked so many times.

It sounds like I made it up, but the spy plane is absolutely real. Maggie wasn't imagining things. The RAAF base in Laverton in Melbourne's west reported the plane, and it was seen over the Melbourne docks, Williamstown, South Melbourne and Port Melbourne. And it wasn't the only enemy spy plane to fly over Australia, taking notes and photographs.

I know that we don't follow this story to the end of the war. I like to think that everyone came home safely, especially Pat. But, sadly, so many people didn't, and if you've ever heard of the Kokoda Track in Papua New Guinea, you'll know that there were very tough times ahead for Australians fighting there.

But Maggie's prayer did come true. The war did

finally end in 1945. Australia, Japan, Germany and Italy have been at peace with each other ever since. And I'm off to watch St Kilda play in the AFLW. I bet that would blow Maggie's mind!

Oh, and one more thing. When I was a kid, there was a nun at my primary school called Sister Johanna. At lunchtime she would dazzle us with her footy skills. Her torpedo kicks were the best I'd ever seen!

For years, right into my adulthood, I often found myself wondering where Sister Johanna was and how she was doing. Well, in 2018, at a writers' festival in Queensland, I was approached by a woman who had come to sit in on one of my sessions.

And, yes . . . it was Sister Johanna! She was surprised that I remembered her, but I told her how I couldn't forget someone who was so inspirational to so many of us kids, and how she was my very first footy hero. She was my Sister Clare.

I hope you enjoyed this story, and the next time you kick a footy or watch an AFL Women's game, you'll think of the unstoppable Flying Flanagan.

Since the war began there are German soldiers on every corner, fearsome gangsters and the fascist police everywhere. But when Antonio decides to trust a man who has fallen from the sky, he leaps into an adventure that will change his life . . . and maybe the future of everyone in Sicily.

When the river rises and the city of Paris begins to disappear under water, Frederic decides to help those who can't help themselves. But as his heroic acts escalate, so does the danger. But as the waters subside, can he find justice for his father and find out what courage really means?

When Peter's family leaves for a trip across the border, he stays behind. So when the government builds a wall through the city, guarded by soldiers, tanks and ferocious dogs, he's trapped. Peter has a courageous plan . . . It would be a great escape, but can he survive it?